MY BOOK

OF REVELATIONS

MY BOOK
OF REVELATIONS

IAIN HOOD

RENARD PRESS

RENARD PRESS LTD

124 City Road
London EC1V 2NX
United Kingdom
info@renardpress.com
020 8050 2928
www.renardpress.com

My Book of Revelations first published by Renard Press Ltd in 2023

Cover design by Will Dady

Printed in the United Kingdom by Severn

FSC
www.fsc.org
MIX
Paper | Supporting
responsible forestry
FSC® C022174

CARBON
NEUTRAL

ISBN: 978-1-80447-067-1

9 8 7 6 5 4 3 2 1

MY BOOK

OF REVELATIONS

A city is more than a place in space, it is a drama in time.

Sir Patrick Geddes, FRSE

Dear _____, I'll gie ye some advice,
You'll tak it no uncivil:
You shouldna paint at angels mair,
But try and paint the devil.

To paint an Angel's kittle wark,
Wi' Nick, there's little danger:
You'll easy draw a lang-kent face,
But no sae weel a stranger.

Robert Burns, 'To An Artist'

That most ingenious of human inventions, the spoked wheel that turns independently of its axle, had scarcely been seen before in Scotland. Accordingly, when a chaise penetrated to the north no Apollo's chariot could have created more amazement, and men bowed low before the driver in the belief that none but the owner would be permitted to drive so magnificent a vehicle. Several new stage routes came into existence. The coach between Glasgow and the capital began to make four miles an hour instead of the former three. Once a month passengers of sufficient wealth and daring could set out from the Grassmarket in Edinburgh with a fair chance of reaching London sixteen days later.

Catherine Carswell, The Life of Robert Burns

Everything's connected to everything else... if you want it to be.

Kirov Tzucanari, Notebooks

1

15 centuries to go

The genius monk Dionysius Exiguus moved to Rome at about the age of thirty, already convinced he had to end the chaos of the various calendars which started from a multiplicity of years 1. There were ones he may not have known that well, like the Vikram Samvat, a lunisolar calendar used by Hindus which counted from Emperor Vikramaditya of Ujjain's victory over the Saka, though he was a fantastically well-rounded scholar. He would have been familiar with the old Hebrew calendar that counted the years from the destruction of the Temple. From within his own European and specifically Roman traditions he certainly knew the most notable calendar in Europe counted from the putative year of *ab urbe condita*, the founding of Rome, giving rise to the AUC calendar. But too often calendars were of regnal years, those which counted the number of years a sovereign, pontiff or consul had been on his – mostly his – or her throne, or the year elected to consular office. These calendars were regional and not related to the most important historical event in the history of humankind from Dionysius's perspective, as a Christian monk, the *anno Domini nostri Jesu Christi*, the year it was since the birth, or conception, or incarnation

– there is some debate about which he meant, and what 'incarnation' entailed – of his Lord God, Jesus Christ.

The search was on for the *anno Domini nostri Jesu Christi*. Using mathematics of various and inventive sorts that we won't go into just now, Dionysius was able to calculate, about 25 years after he had begun his efforts, that he was, in fact, in the year AD 525, and that thus his strenuous attempt to solidify the birth or conception or incarnation of Jesus as the premiere and ultimate pivotal point in human history had begun in AD 500. The time we now call before Christ, BC, or before the Common Era, BCE, was decisively put to bed with the change over from 1 BC to AD 1.

There is no year 0 in Dionysius Exiguus's calendar: the year AD 1 follows on directly from the year 1 BC. Like much of the mathematics of the mainly Greek mathematicians that Dionysius relied upon, he was himself likely to have had philosophical reasons for opposing the idea that zero could be any sort of natural number at all.

Almost all previous calendars ran from year 1, since noting the first year of a sovereign's reign or first year on from some significant event makes sense; but counting the year previous to this as the sovereign's or event's zero year makes none. We will return to the implications of this decision, the lack of a zero year in the AD calendar, in due course. And, of course, we must consider all these dates to be heavily caveated with '*circa*'.

For many reasons, counting systems themselves during these times had inbuilt limits of confidence, as did the provenance of source material time markers, the Gospels of Luke and Matthew, whence so much guesstimate work grew, were contradictory and internally inaccurate, suggesting, for example, that Jesus was 27 when he began his ministry and therefore 30 when he was crucified, died and resurrected, and

2

was born sometime between 6 BC and 4 BC, as opposed to what might have been implied by *anno Domini*: 1 BC, 30 and 33 years, with Jesus conceived and incarnate at the Annunciation on the 25th of March, 1 BC, gestated for the usual human term of nine months, and therefore born and incarnated on the 25th of December 1 BC. The sharp-eyed among us will note some slipperiness with the concept of incarnation, specifically the Incarnation, and the start date for 1 AD here. For much of this, approximation and fairly rough calculation is all we have. All such calendars of the time, not least the *anno Mundi*, were fraught with such difficulties.

If you were to have asked Jesus himself – when alive as a man on earth, that is – what year it was, several answers were available to him. As a Galilean he may have said he was living in some tens of years, depending on what age he was, into the reign of the Tetrarch Herod Antipas. As a Jew, he may have said it was in the Jewish calendar year 3780 or 90 or so, again dependent on his age. As a citizen of the Roman Empire, he may have said he was in one of the years of a certain Consulship or Consulships, or in some regnal year of, mostly, the reign of Tiberius Caesar Augustus, or in the AUC years 754 to 784ish. He even may have heard tell of the Vikram Samvat from traders, say, trading along the developing Silk Road or the established spice-trade routes. He didn't care much what year he was in, I suspect, Jesus, as mostly he thought he was in the end times, after which the Kingdom of God would supersede the earthly world.

By the 9th century, AD was also to comprehensively trump use of *anno Mundi*, the calendar that counted from a literal reading of the creation of the universe – the 'world' in ancient parlance – in the Old Testament. This was part of Dionysius Exiguus's mission: AD 500 was also the year *anno Mundi* 6000, which, enthusiastic end-of-the-worldists believed, was to be the year the Apocalypse would be upon them: risen dead, return of Christ, end of everything, et cetera. And yet here he was, Dionysius, and so was the world, after the 1st of January in the year AD 525, AM 6025, twenty-five years after no noticeable apocalypse.

The AUC and AD calendars, with adaptations through first the Julian and then Gregorian calendars, carried along the Roman date for the official appointment of consuls, the first day of January, as the change from old to new year. Though, of course, other new year dates persist, and not just from other cultures, like Chinese New Year. If you don't think so, then do your tax return – calculated according to the fiscal year that runs from the 6th of April one year to the 5th of April the next – on New Year's Eve while thinking wistfully about your pre-work, pre-tax-worries student days, the days that formed an academic year – the one that runs September, Octoberish through to late May, June. De-Christianised as the Common Era calendar, which may have had Dionysius Exiguus spinning in his grave, *anno Domini* would go on to conquer the world, with the People's Republic of China even choosing to use it for domestic purposes – they had used it for international trading since 1912 – from 1949 onwards.

Dionysius Exiguus died *circa* AD 544, and therefore about 1,405 years before this final triumph of his calendar.

2

15 decades to go

By the year 1850, developments in travel and communication made apparent that local time usage, by which all geographical points defined noon as the time at which the sun reached its highest point overhead, could no longer be sustained. Up until about then, no one moved fast enough nor far enough for time differences to matter. But, for example, the first temporary train terminus of the Great Western Railway had been opened at Paddington in 1838, and since 1840 GWR had used portable precision time pieces, chronometers, set to Greenwich Mean Time, to help with the running of their trains, expected periods of time for the train to travel east or west counted with a single point of reference and therefore the times at which the train would reach intermediate stations and a final terminus. By 1847 most railway companies in the United Kingdom of Great Britain and Ireland – we'll use the terms of the time – were using GMT as the time throughout the nation for their own purposes and on their timetables. Yet local time still prevailed in many people's minds over the curious London-centric imposition of GMT, what people who cared to be bothered by it called 'railway time'. Similarly, the development of telegraphy meant that, by 1852, the Post Office could transmit the time from the Observatory at Greenwich, and soon most if not all public clocks, or noting of the time via other public means, such as church bells, were using GMT, though often with secondary means of noting the local and therefore 'real' time. Some realised it could only be a matter of time before the whole world would require such standardised time. And it was a whole new world. Momentous events were taking place in all areas of life. For example, in 1859, Darwin finally published... Yes, OK, we all know that side of things.

(It's possible you're pushing it.)

In 1868, New Zealand, at the time still governed as a colony, even though the Constitution Act of 1852 had established a fairly independent New Zealand parliament, adopted a standardised time of GMT+11.30. By 1880 the bulk of the British Isles were using GMT rather than local times, spreading out to the Isle of Man, Jersey and Guernsey, and, finally, Ireland, which in 1880 set Dublin Mean Time, measured at the Dunsink Observatory as GMT minus 25 minutes and 21 seconds. In 1916, GMT superseded Dublin Mean Time. The first inklings of time zones were being established.

During these same years a number of schemes for a worldwide system of time zones were proposed. The foremost of these was developed by the Italian mathematician Quirico Filopanti in the 1850s, whose system went unrecognised and was never adopted, and then in 1876 by Kirkcaldy-born Scots-Canadian Sir Sandford Fleming, who was instrumental in the invention of twenty-four one-hour time zones, and the setting of Greenwich as the prime meridian – the zero degree by which each part of the earth relates longitudinally by degrees. Not to say he was alone in this endeavour, and indeed there were a number of learned committees and political appointees who took a more or less useful part in these developments. In one sense, Fleming might be considered one of the great obliterators of time: he banished all the other GMT+ and GMT-s of interim minutes – the

6

GMT-s of 5.45, 1.23, 9.58 and the GMT+s of 7.38, 3.46, 6.21 – leaving only 1, 2, 3, et cetera.

It was this eminent Victorian, Sir Sandford Fleming FRSC KCMG, who, travelling in Ireland in 1876, missed a train in Dublin one day, due to an error on the timetable between A.M. and P.M. that obviously irritated the illustrious gentleman greatly. The already reputed 'most distinguished Canadian of his age' was then forced to spend a night at the train station. He arrived with twenty minutes to spare for the scheduled 5:35 P.M. train. Unfortunately the train had arrived on schedule too, at 5:35 A.M., the P.M. printed in the timetable being the offending error. As he was left waiting for the next available train, Fleming conceived of a simpler world with a simpler clock, one that would consider all twenty-four hours of the day without the fraught-with-risk possibilities of double-counting the hours in the day. As he thought it through it became clearer and clearer to him that it was only stupidity that kept us from counting past the number twelve in this particular instance. In time, he would go on to not only proposing a twenty-four clock, but also a twenty-four hour terrestrial time that would map over the earth in twenty-four hour intervals, beginning with a prime meridian, proceeding by fifteen longitude degrees around the globe, and define the hour in these geographical locales relative to… oh, let's say… the time at the zero hour at Greenwich.

(Well, there you go – a ripple of applause and laughter, and in a job-interview presentation, of all things.)

Thanks.

At the International Meridian Conference held in Washington D.C. in 1884, convened at the bequest of one of the, perhaps unfairly, lesser-known presidents of the United States, the 21st president, President Chester A. Arthur, the adoption of Greenwich as the internationally recognised prime meridian and the intention to adopt a time-zone scheme much like Fleming's were confirmed. Over the coming years, the rail companies pushing west over the States, bringing scientific, political and commercial interests to bear, set out time zones across the land, which were more rough-hewn and less universally adopted than one might hope – certainly more than the precision-minded Fleming might have hoped – but which were, nonetheless, for the most part, workable.

The ingredients for a worldwide and universally agreed set of time zones, based for the most part on Fleming's principles, if not quite the detail, were all now to hand. This would lead, in time, to the creation of Coordinated Universal Time, UTC, where UTC zero-maps directly on to GMT. The Greenwich prime meridian would denote the middle of the first, zero, hour, with positive and negative offsets running to respectively left and right of the zero, if viewed on a map, or thought of as running anticlockwise as conceived of viewed looking down upon the north pole, and thus the farthest reaches of the offset meet at the opposite side of the spinning earth from Greenwich zero at the point the nominally UTC-12 nominally meets the nominally UTC+12, at the 180th degree. This point is also called the international date line, as it is the point at which one day changes over into another, so that to differentiate those in zone UTC-12 from those in UTC+12, those in UTC-12 are in the next calendar day to those in UTC+12. In practice, and for certain geographical reasons, not least the spread-out nature of atolls and islands in the Pacific Ocean comprising one geopolitical entity, and the nature of the time at which these entities wished sunrise and sunset to be considered, such date-line changes could happen at UTC-10 and UTC+14 or UTC-11 and UTC+13, Kiribati being one such trans-date-line nation.

The 32 atolls that make up the Republic of Kiribati in the Pacific Ocean lie across the international date line. This raised an interesting dilemma for the approximately 120,000 people of the Republic – though I don't know why, apart from the constant river of births and deaths, it shouldn't be possible to get a fairly accurate exact number of Kiribatians since they inhabit a fairly contained space and there just aren't that many of them: could be counted on one day, really – I suppose it comes down to the day you pick. They, or some of them, or someone among them realised, in the run-up to the turn of the millennium – let's leave aside whether this was the turn of the millennium for now – New Year's Eve 1999 into New Year's Day 2000, that as they straddled the international date line, this also meant they could technically jump to one side or the other. Perhaps perceiving the note taken – primacy- over recency-wise – in media coverage of new-year celebrations, Kiribati, not without controversy and mostly due to their unilateral decision, moved from one side to the other, from UTC-11 to UTC+13 and UTC-10 to UTC+14 across the islands at midnight on the 30th December 1994, skipping out on a day, and landing in the moments after midnight on the 1st of January 1995 ahead of the rest of the world as opposed to the last to experience the delights of a New Year's Eve and morning shindig.

Although there has been other time-zone jiggery-pokery here and there, most often with whole nations choosing the same time zone across their east-to-west expanse, or a nation choosing to be in one time zone over another for political reasons, for the most part, the system that runs closely to Fleming's principles has held up admirably, with the scheme now universally applied, as it had to become throughout the 20th century, as, again, developments in transportation and communications made an agreed time that applied world-wide an ever greater necessity, reaching to all the nations of the earth, last but not least, Nepal. It is possible that one

9

Victorian gentleman's irritation and time spent in a Dublin train station, bored, thoughtful, feeding his anger with the facts of the matter regarding time, trains, train timetables and the blithering idiots who misprinted P.M. when A.M. was so patently what they meant never had such far-reaching consequences as did Sir Sandford Fleming's irritation at a faulty Dublin train timetable. I imagine him in his high Victorian grandeur, frock-coated, top-hatted, pince-nezzed and big-bearded, shoving some poor soul sandwichboardman carrying a sandwichboard proclaiming THE END IS NIGH as he made his way towards some other poor dolt of a ticket seller or other railwayman of the Dublin, Wicklow and Wexford Railway Company and sniffily saying, 'The end *will* be nigh for someone when I catch the Irish idiot who printed this timetable!'

(You probably are pushing the possibility of their boredom.)

Nepal, that seemingly ever-otherworldly country, that somehow timeless world unto itself, was the last to adopt the UTC system, moving from the local mean solar time set in the nation's capital Kathmandu of 5 hours, 41 minutes and 16 seconds ahead of GMT/UTC, first joining Indian Standard Time of UTC+5.30 in 1920, then having a wee square-peg, round-hole moment in 1986 sort of typical of this minnow that sits between two whales, creating Nepal Standard Time of UTC+5.45. This all as more people travelled to and communicated with the country, no doubt, and in the foment of nascent Nepalese pro-democracy movements that sought to bring an end to King Birendra's oppressive Panchayat partyless government's political system. It also can't be a coincidence that these years were also notable for the development of worldwide computer systems and networks, which were soon to be the main conduit of the peoples of the world communicating with each other.

3

15 years to go

1985. Let me remind you. Ronald Reagan. Mikhail Gorbachev. Ronald Reagan *and* Mikhail Gorbachev. Margaret Thatcher doing everything she could to crush the unions here. Ooh. An ooh? That's not controversial, is it? Maybe I don't know... your generation... Not that I'm assuming a generation for you lot... Maybe my politics is a bit dinosaur. Anyway. Plane crashes, terrorist attacks and fires. Trouble in the Middle East. *Eastenders* in the UK and *Neighbours* in Australia and *Moonlighting* in the States. The IRA. An earthquake in Chile. The Lebanese Civil War and the Beirut hostage takings. Islamic Jihad blowing up a café in Madrid. *Amadeus* and *The Killing Fields* and, right up our thematic street, *Back to the Future*.

(A whoop? These idiots don't even know that *Peggy Sue Got Married* is so much better. The year after.)

The Mujahideen. The end of a ban on interracial marriage in South Africa. New Coke. The death of New Coke. Bradford City stadium fire and Heysel Stadium, the injury and deaths of fans of games of football. The hole in the ozone layer. Bombings in Nepal. The *Rainbow Warrior* sunk in Auckland harbour by the French secret service. Live Aid. And 'We Are the World' by USA for Africa. A state of emergency in South Africa due to protests in black townships. A massacre in Peru. The plane crash killing Samantha Smith.

The locating of the Titanic. An earthquake in Mexico. The death of Klinghoffer on the *Achille Lauro*. A siege in Bogotá, Colombia. Kasparov versus Karpov. A volcano erupts in Colombia killing tens of thousands. Terrorist attacks, assault rifles, grenades, at Rome and Vienna airports. And Dian Fossey was murdered in Rwanda. She worked with mountain gorillas, trying to figure out whether they had language or something. You might have seen the film based on her book, or, who knows, read her book, *Gorillas in the Mist*. And now I'm remembering something, might have been to do with Fossey, that after years of studying gorillas they did work out what they were saying to each other, that ninety-nine point nine nine per cent of the time what they were saying was, Hello, hi, hey, hi, hello, I'm over here, and now I'm here, I'm me. Doesn't make them that different from us, really, does it? The other zero point zero one per cent of the time they were asking who was holding the banana stash.

Now, to some other things I didn't know at the time, but have found out since. First, on the 1st of January 1985, the Internet's Domain Name System was created. Did you know this? Well, I know you know all about the Domain Name System. I meant, did you know it was created on the 1st of January 1985? I mean, all memory gets misty. And I'm sure you know the implications of the creation of the Domain Name System. I won't be going into that. And in the States, Microsoft released Windows 1.0 – how about that? I'm sure I don't have to go into the history and implications of that for our purposes! Windows 1.0. It must have been quite a moment. But was there an even bigger moment in computing that year? Yes, that's right. You're a smart crowd! The publication of the first edition of *The C++ Programming Language*. By Danish genius Bjarne Stroustrup. Mm. I just like trying to say his name. Stroustrup? Bjarne?

Bjarne? And I know that, for you lot, I don't have to say any more about this development. And then there was the formation of the National Science Foundation Network, or NSFNET, with the linking of five supercomputer centres across the United States, at Princeton, Pittsburgh, University of California at San Diego, University of Illinois at Urbana-Champaign and Cornell University. Some bunch of hippies start the connected Bulletin Board System and start calling themselves an online community. Dell sold his first computer, PageMaker for Mac was released, kickstarting the publishing revolution, and Nintendo gave us – wow, am I getting a whoop for that? – Nintendo gave us the Nintendo Entertainment System and we all met Mario the Plumber! Another whoop?! Well, OK.

(The slip from formal to informal all going well. Pull them in. You have to know how to handle dweeboids, geekboys, Hobbits, nerds. Or is that herd nerds?)

1985 was also when Jobs lost out and got kicked out of Apple. On a darker note, outside his computer rental shop, a sign of the times itself... Well, Dell's computer was selling at $795.00, which was a lot of money in 1985, and rental was the way to go – the same way television and even radio rental had been in the past. Yes, even radios. Haven't you heard of Radio Rentals? Yes, that was a radio-rental company! Because in, I don't know, the 1920s and 30s a radio would have cost you more than your house, I'm guessing. We're getting off the point. Outside his computer-rental shop, Hugh Scrutton was the first fatality in a bombing campaign of domestic terrorism. He was blown up by an explosive device placed there by Ted Kaczynski. Oh! Yes, we've all seen *Good Will Hunting*, haven't we! We all love a story of a maths genius. I mean Will, not Ted, there. Yes, the Unabomber.

(Don't let them blow you off course again like that.)

And PlayNet, Inc. in Troy, New York State created the PlayNet online service, which allowed Commodore 64 users to game together remotely and chat via electronic messenger, or what we might call mail – electronic mail, or e-mail, as it would become known. PlayNet licenced the system to Control Video Corporation, which would change name to Quantum Computer Services, which in turn would later change its name to… Yeah, you're right, America Online, subsequently styled AOL. The *online* world would, over the next fifteen years, become a place, a cyberspace, which has its own time zone, or zones, and, with the ability for people to communicate instantaneously over huge geographical areas, in whatever time zone they are in in the real world, its own spacelessness and timelessness. A world equivalent and opposite to the real world, IRL or 'in real life'. That dull, dirty, grey place we're forced to make our way through in boring real time. *Offline*. But surely being *on* is better than being *off*, right? It just sounds right, doesn't it? Now, we can debate the realness of the online world, where we can make real decisions that have real consequences, and increasingly we know people can make bad decisions with really bad consequences. But anyway, our concern is that the time, the changing time in the abstract, in our systems and online, can have an effect in our real world, and our question is, what will that effect be?

(OK. Pulled back to where you wanted to be. Thank you, James Burke. Back in those days. *The Day the Universe Changed*. *Connections* when I was 12, 13.)

I think that gives us enough to know why we are where we are. I look forward to the technical interview in – three, is it? Two. Two days. Gentlemen. And ladies. Does anyone have any questions?

(Told the company had 'interests' in whisky, agrichemicals, pharmaceuticals and computers themselves. The CEO a

14

millionaire several times over. His eccentricity: don't take offence, they said. No oil in there? I asked. Do not bring that up if you meet him. Well, OK. You mean he won't be here at the presentation today? Probably not. Possibly, but probably not. He's possibly in the Caribbean at the moment.)

What else can we say about 1985? The first year that we actually lived through. We – you and I – can actually *remember* 1985. No one here under 14? No, I suspected not. There are things I have mentioned that I remember about 1985, but I'll admit for much of this I went to the library and looked up headlines. That's the way we know things, isn't it? For the time being, anyway. We'll get to that, maybe during the technical…

(Old man arriving at the back door. You're late, mate.)

Yes. There are certain personal experiences I do remember from 1985. Waking up on New Year's Day, for example, with the same earworm playing in my head that would play in many people's heads, certainly in the UK, that year: 'Do They Know It's Christmas?', the 'Feed the World' end section. Yes? You too? And you? Mmm. As I say, all of us at some point that year. And the Live Aid concert. 13th of July 1985. I wasn't there, but I spent the day at a barbecue at a then-girlfriend's parents' house in Ayr, balancing catching a burger or hotdog with watching most of the hours and hours of coverage of the concert, into the small hours, right through to the end.

Will we wrap this up here?

(Look around. Movement. Unclenching. Prince released his song '1999' for the first time in 1982, alongside the album *1999*. But it was rereleased in the UK in 1985 as a twelve inch – it was one of us, probably Andy, that had it, but we all played it – we're gonna… That New Year's Eve? Probably, at the Pavilion. Whatever year it was, '1999' was a New Year's song. A gift to DJs, easy floor filler. It looked to the future then. On New Year's Eve 1985 it was probably too far in the future,

1999, to really or fully conceive of. We'd be 35 or thereabouts. That was old. We were twenty-year-olds. 35 was for ever away, almost your life again. But was it? I don't specifically remember being there that New Year's. But they are the kinds of things, the repetitions of life, that can roll into one another. You spent one New Year here a few times, there some other times, once before in Edinburgh at the big event, but which year was which? Even the unique one, Edinburgh? I mean, what specific year was that. 1994? 95? 93? Close as I can pin it down.)

Is that…? Is that OK?

(Forming into small groups, chatting. How many are actually in here? Why did they want a presentation to the whole company, anyway? My mother's friend, a fan from the sixties and seventies – fifties as well – expressing her homophobia by saying she could not forgive Rock Hudson. And now I wonder what it was she could not forgive. Yes, literally him, Rock, she could not forgive *him*. But what? Couldn't forgive him for dying? Couldn't forgive him for being gay? Or she couldn't forgive that only recently she had found out he was gay? Or worse, in this sense: had been gay through her years of dreaming of him as her – sexual? – partner? During the last year, when he became the first celebrity to disclose an AIDS diagnosis, and promptly died not long after this. She sold the VHS video collection. And Milan Kundera was who we were all reading. *The Unbearable Lightness of Being* was just starting to circulate. But it was *The Book of Laughter and Forgetting* that we had all been passing between us. Love a book with *Book* in the title, me. I remember the shock of recognition of a new thought when at the back of the copy we had there's an interview between Philip Roth and the author. Roth kicks off, preparing for some point he is about to make about Kundera's philosophy, asking Kundera if he thinks the end of the world is coming. Kundera asks when Roth is thinking of, and Roth replies something like, Imminently, to which Kundera notes that the idea the whole show was about to end is an idea almost as old as the human species. Oh, so nothing to worry about, says Roth. And this is the kicker. Kundera says something like, What? No! If humanity has been thinking this for as long as it's been around there must be something to it!)

Any other questions? Perhaps over coffee?

(No one listening. This one has come to stand by me but is saying nothing to me. Just kind of *hanging* there. We could all be dead by the morning. To think I had almost forgotten those years' end of the world. Sign of the times. That apocalypse. The big disease with the little name. In 1985 the virus didn't even have an agreed name. Just 'the disease'. AIDS. Gay Plague. Jesus. The danger that was a threat to us all. The Tombstone Monolith, the Iceberg. What we knew, just as an adult sex life beckoned and was upon us was that sex could kill again. A double end to the world as we had known it. So that was the gist of the song. Party *now*. NOW. *NOW!* Free your mind and your ass will follow. Make my funk the P-Funk. The Subclub in Jamaica Street. And for Prince and all us dancers that would be the big one, the party of the millennium! 2000. The day the earth still stood. Or was destroyed. But it was New Year's, and did Neil say something about champagne? But. I told him it just wouldn't be right. I didn't think it would. Because it wasn't New Year, was it? And it was when '1999' came on and we were dancing like we could die tomorrow that suddenly the choke rose up my throat and it all went wrong from there. Something about the lyrics? Something about partying? We were young. Too young. You all looked so young – that was what one of the mothers said at the funeral the day before that night, the reason we were all gathered together back in Ayr when by rights we should have been in Glasgow or Edinburgh, getting on with our courses. I was standing on some street outside a Glasgow University department department, can't remember exactly where now, Patrick standing next to me, and another student, a young woman, from the year below you at school, Sharon if I remember correctly, from the house on Hillhead Street, approached and said, Your dad phoned. She meant the communal phone in the flat – my father had called me on that phone. Stone-age technology. 1985. I smiled. Beyond impossible. What would my dad be calling me on that phone for? Then she said, Brad Stevenston died. My bag fell from my left hand and I remember grabbing it in its fall to the ground with my right hand. A ridiculous – ludicrous, Brad would have said, one of his favourite words – detail. And my initial thought was, Why would my dad have told this person more than for me to call him back, as though I was affronted by the disclosure of too personal a detail from my own life. Beyond ludicrous. My father and this young woman had done nothing wrong. Your friend is dead. Twenty. Close enough.)

Well, OK. Thanks, everyone, for giving me this chance.

(Perhaps it isn't right to mine your memories and the lives of your friends in this way. Did it go OK? Think so. How are you going to get through the technical? Leave that for now. Preparations. Good old *Encyclopaedia Britannica* CD-ROM. Thank God I didn't start, as I had thought to, with 15,000 years to go – humans – 150,000 years to go – fishing and ornaments – 1,500,000 years to go – fire, tools – 15,000,000 years to go – hominids – 150,000,000 years to go – mammals, flowers, pollinators – 1,500,000,000 – eukaryotes, Metazoa – 15,000,000,000 – nothing happening at all – much like, with the end of history and all that, our current times. In no time there was nothing nowhere. I had not thought to walk down this road again, not this early, just kind of unexpected, in my book.)

4

15 months to go

(During the opportunity for coffee and informal chat I was asked two questions of more substance than just the How's the coffee? Do you want a biscuit? sort. First, one of the people from the front row of the audience for the presentation spoke up.)

You said that for much of the information in your presentation you went to the library and looked up headlines… But that that's the way we know things *for the time being*. What did you mean by *for the time being*?

Well, I had been in a library, I said, looking up headlines, but not by looking at old copies of newspapers. I searched a CD-ROM of the *Encyclopaedia Britannica*, using a computer.

(Remember that picture of Bill Gates suspended at the top of two immense towers of paper pages to represent the information that could then be put on a CD-ROM after he had… invented it? Hey, I just looked it up on a CD-ROM! I looked up CD-ROM on the *Encyclopaedia Britannica* CD-ROM. I'd say that Gates in that photograph is probably celebrating an increase in storage capacity or something. Because that picture is from well after it was invented — not by Gates, though Microsoft had creative input, I think from the start of its development, the formatting of it and stuff.)

And anyway, I said, I didn't really look at headlines from 1985. I mostly just looked up notable events in 1985. You can do that with a CD-ROM. So really 'library' and 'headlines' were being used metaphorically. I'm not sure that there are all the words we need for how we'll sift and search for information in the future, but I do know that libraries filled with old copies of print newspapers are starting to feel a bit dead to me already. Probably books'll be next.

(I could see I was getting a few 'futurologist' vibes from the audience members. Push it, I thought.)

And I'm sure the CD-ROM isn't where things will stop. It's already an almost obsolete tech. I mean, we have a working World Wide Web, we all know about Yahoo! and AOL and Netscape. There's a bookselling site that's growing a bit, called Amazon, and I hear there's a much better way of searching coming soon, called the Google. After that, there will be an explosion of information online. Communities will form, and networking will be online, like Theglobe.com and GeoCities. There'll be a dot-com bubble, no doubt, and, like all bubbles, this one will burst. But in the future (I was thinking of Patrick) our lives will be lived in a virtual way, shopping, meeting people socially, sharing our thoughts, knowledge, skills. Our loves. And our hatreds. All online. And there'll be an online encyclopaedia, unlike anything seen before, with vast, vast amounts of information… (The old man who was late had joined us: late again, mate.) Almost a Tower of Babel of knowledge, a labyrinth, a mirror of everything in reality, an incomprehensible, unmappable amount of knowledge… (I wasn't finished, but I was interrupted.)

And what did you mean about coming back to the year 2000 being the millennium? said one of the panel – not the late, old man.

Oh, I just mean, with there being no year zero between 1 BC and AD 1, there's some debate, isn't there, as to whether 1999 into 2000 is the millennium or 2000 into 2001 is the millennium. Do you see what I mean? (A few nodded, a few shook their heads.) Well, I mean, a millennium is a thousand years, isn't it? So, the first millennium was AD 1 to AD 1000, right? Am I right? And the second millennium would then be AD 1001 to AD 2000, right? A thousand years for each. So it'll be 2000 into 2001 that actually… Really, for it to be 1999 into 2000, the thousand years would be, for the first millennium, 1 BC to AD 999, second millennium AD 1000 to AD 1999. Do you see?

(The old man came forward.) Tell me, he said, do you think the world will end at the millennium, whenever it is, next year or the next? he said. For us, this company, I mean, with Y2K?

The idea that the end of the world is coming is, has been and probably will be, then and after then, one that has been prevalent in human society since it began, I said.

So, the apocalypse is coming, he said.

Well, I said, the apocalypse is always coming.

So, you don't think there's any validity in the idea? Since, after all, we're all still here. (He swept his hand around the room.)

What makes you think that? I said. If an idea has been prevalent in the whole history of human existence, then I say there must be something to it! For example, I hear a lot about how the development of artificial intelligence, and it's here, in your networks and in your products, will reach an apotheosis, or is that an apocalypse, when the machines and networks become self-aware. Well, I say, what if the apocalypse comes because we finally make machines that make us, the humans, unable to be self-aware, unable to tell the real world from the virtual, blank to the possibility that we are living through or even have lived through the apocalypse, it's just that we haven't even noticed it happening?

(I waited for someone to casually say that I was quoting or paraphrasing Kundera, and then going on to express a dull thought that many of them had had. We had all been reading Kundera back in the eighties. The room suddenly stilled. The old, late man's arms had fallen to his side and he was smiling. He was such an unassuming presence that I felt surprised that all eyes were now on him, including my own. His eyes crinkled with crow's feet as he smiled.)

I'm not sure we need a technical interview, he said.

(What is this? I thought. Who is he, anyway? Then, of course, it hit me full-force that he was Toby Mole, the CEO of the very company I was standing in, Molextrics. Already Scotland's first and only tech multimillionaire, the financial wizard, the inventor of something intrinsic to every bank transfer in the world. The recluse, the photo-shy, the some-would-say-eccentric, the famously beyond-humble Toby Mole. And he had said what?)

I want you on staff. You know the depth, Mole said.

(How does he know? He arrived late. He had to be Mole. It was suddenly obvious on the faces of everyone in there. I had to be sure.)

Mr... Mole? I said.

Mm, of course. You know the depth. (The depth of what?) Thanks, I said.

Mm, Mole repeated. The depth. I've heard enough.

Are you absolutely sure? I said.

(Mole looked around at one adviser after another.) We do have references, don't we? he said. (No one moved for a moment.) We do have references, is this correct? (Finally, there was some nodding.) And they all check out? he said.

22

(Advisers were looking at each other, back at Mole, back at each other, with Mole growing more red-faced, frustrated, an angry God of the Old Testament, what with the hair and the beard.) Well? he said. (There was a shuffling of paper as though this legitimised anything.)

Yeses echoed around the room.

Good. Then I've heard enough, Mole said.

(And then the room was breaking up and disintegrating, people flowing away to fulfil Mole's wishes, whatever they were understood to be. It left me and Mole standing in a pretty minimally staffed room. He was staring at me and it looked to me as though he was nodding. Then there seemed to be only me and him.)

You're worried? he said.

It's just, well, I would rather prove myself, I said.

You can, if you like. You know this man, Jaron Lanier?

Of course, I said.

You know him?

I shrugged. Who doesn't?

You've met him, perhaps? Mole said.

A laugh escaped me. No, not that, I said. Though of course I would have loved to.

I've just been with him, Mole said. We met in New York.

Really? I said.

Lanier? Of course. We had a lot to talk about.

(We had wandered back over to the table with the coffee on it. Mole poured himself more and held up the pot to offer me more, but I declined.)

Well, of course, Mole said, if you know his work… He's a visionary. He's the one who invented the term 'virtual reality'.

I'm fairly certain that was Artaud in *The Theatre and Its Double*. (I said this before I thought that perhaps contradicting

23

my new boss was a bad idea. Mole stopped moving, frozen in the moment.) Of course, I said, Artaud is French and said it in French, so maybe Lanier was the, um, inventor of the term in English.

Are you saying 'are toad'? 'Our toad'? I can't quite catch what you are saying.

Oh, it's nothing important, really…

Jaron Lanier, to get back to my point, not only invented the term 'virtual reality', he's also making it a reality. He is able to construct virtual realities.

He's obviously a genius, yes, I said.

He's working on a project just now, Internet2.

Ha, I laughed. Are we done with the first Internet already?

(Mole narrowed his eyes. I had said the wrong thing again. To be honest, it wasn't exactly unheard of.)

Then Mole said, I think I like you even more now. I'm sure we're making the right decision. I see a lot of Jaron in you – you have… (Mole looked me up and down) similar hair, he said, and smiled.

(I was wearing my hair in a fairly typical way for Edinburgh at the time, so I just nodded.)

And a similar something about yourself as Jaron. I like your reference points. Artaud and all that.

Yes, I amn't actually saying 'are toad' or 'our toad'.

I know who Antonin Artaud is, Mole said, lifting his coffee cup to his lips and smiling again.

(Already I was getting the feeling that whatever it was going to be, working for Mole was not going to be dull.)

Did you know he's a musician as well? Mole said.

Artaud? I said. Well…

Lanier, he said.

Oh yes, I said, of course. He's visionary, a Renaissance man.

24

Yes, Mole said, Yer genuine Scots polymath.

Oh, he's Scottish? I asked.

No. Lanier? Sounds more French. He's an American.

Of course, I said.

In effect he's like a Scots polymath. I see a lot of Jaron in you.

(I looked around the room. Mole had a way of making you focus on him only. A couple of assistants or whoever they were had drifted back in. Mibby they had fixed the thing Mole wanted fixing already. Whatever that was.)

You know Tobias – everyone in the place called him T.S. – Mole. Everyone knows Tobias Mole. The man-child multimillionaire; Scotland's richest person in 1991; the restructuring of his 'business interests' to make him – some say *look like* – not Scotland's richest person in any year since 1991; the humble beginning of the Molextrics electronics company; the largest Scalextric track in the world in his highland cottage – the cottage that is actually a substantial castle built for Mole himself; the rumour of 50 bedrooms in this castle; the accumulated land purchases leading to a continuous estate covering 25,000 hectares, which sought to and did outdo the Balmoral estate's 24,800 hectares; the gigantic penthouse conversion in one of the first warehouse building gentrifications in Edinburgh, as Edinburgh slid towards Leith, from where Mole declaimed long and hard on being a displaced East End Weegie; the naming of Molextrics after his favourite track and racing car toy, Scalextrics; the taking to court of Mole by Scalextrics for brand infringement; the trouncing of Scalextrics and their lawyers by Mole and his lawyers in this brand infringement case; the facts about his interests in electronics and the rumours of his interests in computer hardware, computer software, automobile vehicles, real racing cars, land in both Scotland and overseas, water, desalination, whisky and other spirits, agrichemicals; the rumour that Mole once suggested buying a town in rural Scotland and designing or redesigning all of the civic amenities and utilities of the town, with ownership of all these being in his hands, leading to the 'Technolaird' or 'Tech Laird' epithets; his humble beginnings – in the Ayrshire ex-mining community of Cumnock when Cumnock was still a mining community, through the 1960s and 1970s – the East End Weegie was an adopted persona; the rumours a cartel of shady operators conspired to somehow stop Mole entering the oil business as the Scottish fields were discovered and exploited; the dark rumours of how this cartel did so; the rumours – hinted at by Mole himself in the two interviews he has given since 1991 – of his complete lack of interest in mining; Mole's reported private life being, almost completely, in dispute. Facts: he is Scottish, he is about 65 years of age, from Cumnock, or is Glaswegian, dependent on his mood: see how even these 'facts' slip towards the uncertain; the dark hole of facts, fictions, factions, fractions, et cetera leading commentators, such as there are any, to comments about nominal determination, 'Mole/mole'; the simple surface, quote, I'm just the owner of a small electronics company. We make electronics. The Moletron. The Molector. The Moletaniser, the Moleniser... compared with the overly complex business dealings: a shell company he named 'Shellcompany' – Shell Oil intervened but could not deny him – this housed/was the shell of Smollet Holdings (made up of Molelectonica, Molelectroclinical, Molectrotonical, Molelectrolonica, Molelectrologica, Molelectrolology, Molelectoralonica), while Smollet Land Holding housed three further companies (Smallet Land Holdings, Smellet Land Holdings, Smillet Land Holdings, within which the cottage/castle was held in trust), and finally, within Smullet Holdings (made up of Smullet Holdings Caribbean Limited and Smullet Investments) was the company Molets (a shell for Molets UK and Molets Caribbean (a shell for a company registered in the Cayman Islands called Toby Holdings (made up of Toby Investments (Toby Investments Limited, Toby Properties Cayman Islands, Toby Properties Scotland and Toby Properties Caribbean, which housed Molextrics, which acknowledged that a 'T.S. Moles' (*sic*) was a non-executive director))).

As I made my way from the building, I was thinking about the first exercise we had to complete when I started studying memetics after my undergraduate degree in genetics. I studied genetics at Glasgow University, but had moved to Edinburgh University to study memetics, having grown weary of biological determinism and following an interest in bioinformatics that had increased in the two years since I had graduated. And anyway, in a sense, it was just the route mapped out for me by Dawkins. At the time, I was reading a lot of Kundera, as I've mentioned, who was published by Faber and Faber in the UK, and I tried to formulate a meme – which was what the exercise was – based on the first line of *The Unbearable Lightness of Being*, about the mystery of Nietzsche's concept of eternal recurrence that the book goes on to illuminate and illustrate. But after an hour or so nothing was happening with that. Probably because a meme has to be a tiny or at least smallish package of intellectual thought, and the concept of eternal recurrence, or what Kundera was trying to say about it, proved less than amenable to creating this small-to-tiny package. Then I remembered another Faber writer's mention of light, though not in the same sense as the lightness in Kundera's title, but we make our connections where we can, in a title for a book of short stories which I had not read, but I always loved the title: Ellen Gilchrist's collection, *Light Can Be Both Wave and Particle*, which contains the titular story. And I came up with this:

Meme can be both gene and virus.

I sat back, pretty proud of myself for creating a meme that was about memes. I think the lecturer liked it too, because I found a printed-out text of it on the WALL OF SHAME, which only lecturers and teachers were allowed to add notices to. And even though it was not the best meme, or the one I liked best,

Speech don't come for free,

my meme wasn't up on the WALL OF SHAME because it was shameful, I thought, but because the lecturer had liked it. At least, I think this was the case. The WALL OF SHAME, by the way, was mostly filled with envelopes for post to the department, which was the Department of Memetics – post, that is, on which the addresser had failed utterly to spell correctly a word as simple as 'memetics'. Hence the WALL OF SHAME. Bottom-feeders were, as you might expect, 'Department of Mimetics', 'Department of Mimetiks', 'Department of Mymetics', 'Department of Metics', 'Department of Mimetrics'; then there was a second tier, apparently schooled in some way, of 'Department of Mnemetics', 'Department of Mimemetics'; then came the plain daft, 'Department of Emetics', 'Department of My Metrics', 'Department of Meticmex', 'Department of Mytexmex' (we suspected a joker who knew exactly how to spell memetics), 'Dpt of Mimiticis' (one wag suggested this would be from Georges Perec, famous for writing a novel without the letter 'e', ignoring the fact Perec died in 1982 and the department had only been formed in 1985 as the first – they claimed – university department dedicated to the study of memetics in the world: some thought the word 'dedicated' was doing an awful lot of heavy lifting in this sentence); with a top tier dedicated to the frankly deranged 'Depart of Mentmeticus', 'Dept of Nenetics', 'Department of Heretics'; then a place of honour for correct spellings of memetics, but the incorrect spelling of, well, 'Dpartemnt of Memetics', incorrect word choice of 'Apartment for Memetics'. The top spot for the greatest mangling of the departmental name was 'Dementpart fo Inmatetitics' (again, a joker was considered). Oh, and you should have seen what the next-door department's WALL OF SHAME looked like: they were the Department of Epistemology.

The department only coming into existence, at least semantically so, in 1985 was part of the appeal of my move from hard science to something more linguistical based, and, although there was still quite a bit of hard-headed maths in memetics, my real interest was the cultural and ethnographical side of things. How do ideas get around? This was what I wanted to know.

Memes. Everyone knows about them these days. As one of my lecturers said of DNA being the genetic material, in an attempt to cast our minds back to a time when no one was certain it was, Everyone knows these days that DNA is *the* genetic material... Even my wife knows! He got a laugh for that. It was the early eighties and they'd only just invented thinking about not being sexist. Everyone knows the theory of memes now, that ideas or thoughts, rituals or practices, images or sounds follow evolutionary pathways down through time. They proliferate by replication, come about through mutation, experience natural selection to determine their survival or death. Eventually, there is variation which does not stop evolving, and there is no perfect meme, just as there is no perfect set of genes creating a perfect biological creature, flora or fauna, entity, whatever, and mutation, competition and inheritance goes on its merry way to... somewhere. Somewhere else.

But, somehow, over the years of study, eventually completing a PhD, then in advertising, opinion polling and advisory roles in thinktanks, memetics went stale for me. Genetics had gone the same way. I had grown tired of manipulating mice, as my undergraduate thesis required mouse work, and memetics, specifically the work in advertising and opinion polling that I did using it, left me tired of manipulating people. And, anyway, I had got more and more into the Internet and the World Wide Web – didn't we all? – and that's what led me to this job at Molextrics. Sort of, anyway.

I was well away from the Molextrics building by now, and a memory of the very recent past came back to me – the last thing I had said as I came away from Mole and his people.

Mole asked: This thing about the online world, well, is it the end of the world as we know it, as we've known it?

Oh, yes, absolutely, I said.

And the beginning of a new world? he said.

What makes you think that? I said.

I think I had got away with it. The whole thing. The approach seemed to grab them. Talking to computer people you have to keep up a certain way of talking, a communication no-man's land, no-person's land, where we traverse... this wilderness... in search of... No, wait. Where we build communication... No, wait, I've got it. It's a no-person's land because... because... because what? Right, forget that metaphor. It's not working. When herding nerds, one thing is for sure: it's always good to try to tell them there's a bigger world out there, beyond their screens and before the right now of being in front of and in fact glued to those screens, and after that right now, if they can ever pull themselves out of that other world, the one on their screens.

And out here, in the real world, this was about the time, fifteen months before the actual event, that people started speaking, for now in mostly vague ways, about how they were going to spend the millennium. A lot of this was the usual stuff. Where would the good party be? Should we go to Edinburgh? Obviously this was if you didn't live there. Should we head into town? Obviously, again, this was if you did live in Edinburgh. Should we be in the streets before the castle for the fireworks? Certainly tons of English people, who already lived in Edinburgh and felt a smug sense of rightness about celebrating the New Year here, or who didn't live here, but felt an intuitive pull of 'Scotland' for New Year celebrations, were happy to be planning to be in Edinburgh, as the most English and yet performatively 'Scottish' of towns. I mean, not many people in England were planning to head to Paisley or Kilwinning, Livingston or Bonnyrigg, or... I don't know... Ballachulish, let's face it. And we all started to hear about what preparations this or that business, charity, council, organisation, institution or governmental or non-governmental body were making. Of course, even before the 1998 into 1999 New Year had happened, the talk was of the big one, the biggest ever, in all the usual places the plans were growing, developing, mushrooming into vaster and vaster mad events, spreading across the globe, in Auckland; Sydney Harbour; Hong Kong; Taipei; Red Square in Moscow; Dubai; Paris, London and Edinburgh; Copacabana Beach in Rio; Times Square in New York. This really was going to be the party of the millennium, and we were going to *party*! Whether we liked it or not. Then, even then, the darkness started to creep in. What if... What if the millennium was going to go off with a bang in a different way – a bad way – if something went wrong... People like me started getting employed all over the place. Emergency planning, contingency planning. Disaster planning.

From the more quietly pessimistic there were concerns and worries about networks of computers that may fail gradually, not all at once, that nothing precipitous would happen on the 1st of January, or the 2nd, that this would be something of a non-event, early January, but that after this we would start to see failures in business systems, which would come about over days and weeks, phones failing, electricity outages, energy shortages, slowdowns in air traffic causing backlogs, problems in the manufacturing sector, especially electronic parts and automotive components, could slowly ripple through the world economy, and that the many links in global supply chains would be weakened such that the possibility of a worldwide recession was put at seventy per cent or more.

Only the naïvely optimistic were thought to believe that all these systems would function just fine, fully or in some degraded way that simply would not cause problems. Even these people started thinking they might, you know, or rather you never know, take gas and electricity meter readings, check their bank-account balances, mortgage repayments, as close to millennium midnight as they could, sure there would be miscalculations somewhere or other. And when even the naïvely optimistic start doing stuff like that, it was bound to be the very twinklingest beginning of the end.

5

15 weeks to go

It was about fifteen weeks to go that people started making actual emergency plans for the millennium. And I mean, people started losing their heads. A nurse I knew was told to reinstate paper-based procedures that had only recently, in the last few years, been migrated over to computer systems within the NHS. From that micro to the macro planning of additional morgue space for the people who would die if their life-sustaining electronic equipment failed in a first wave, to the people who would die if their life-sustaining medications became unattainable due to ordering, logistics and delivery failures in a second wave – then all the people who would die in a third wave due to the backlog caused by deaths in the first two waves. Apocalyptic thinking was everywhere.

People were planning ever-more remote places to be for the millennium and the days and weeks afterwards. The fewer nationally supplied amenities – mains water, mains gas, grid-provided electricity – the better. Homes for rent in rural areas with generators were booked solid, probably had been for months or years before by the clear-sighted, visionary, paranoid or frankly insane, take your pick. Uist, Shetland, Sutherland, Galway, all popular with nuts in Glasgow, Edinburgh and Ayr.

Stockpiling started. Canned goods, coffee, tea, dried goods, toilet paper. My God, the toilet paper that was bought! Supermarket shelves emptied, but they started telling everyone they had enough for everyone for weeks to come, months, up to a year in the supply chain – which sounded like a lie, even to the sane – and if everyone didn't just calm the fuck down they would bring in rationing. Not because it was needed, but out of spite for the madness that was building up. The messaging was confused.

People started deciding there was no way they would fly anywhere. Getaways that had been booked three or four years in advance, costing an absolute fortune, were now cheap as chips: prices for flights and hotels went through the floor. Then they went through the roof. Then through the floor again. Nobody knew what to do! The cautious believed they would not reach their correct destination, or at least not at the scheduled time, or both these things, and if they did, hope against hope, get there, they would never get back home within any sensible timeframe. The incautious predicted planes falling from the sky on the stroke of midnight and thereafter until every last plane in the sky was downed. To instil confidence, President Bill Clinton's Y2K Czar, John Koskinen, booked a flight that would be in mid-air during the millennium, and told the world he was one hundred per cent sure he would live through the event and the way he chose to celebrate it. And about the same time, in a first-ever cyberspace 'virtual town-hall' meeting in November 1999, which ran with its fair share of glitches itself, President Clinton answered Cynthia from Arizona's question about citizen preparedness for Y2K by saying that he had heard people were preparing to drive out into the Arizona desert in their pick-ups to avoid the chaos they themselves were predicting, but that he wouldn't be doing so himself. A wave of nervous laughter rippled around the room.

But others were predicting that there would be failures at every economic level, in every region of the world: problems in telecommunications, power generation and transportation; disastrous but unnameable events; pockets of failures or general infrastructure outages, confusion and consequent violence, looting, rioting, gang and tribal warfare as usually well-behaved and law-abiding citizens became crazed survivalists intent on protection or conquest of fuel, water, food, shelter and safety. Americans in particular were said to be stocking up on food, water and, of course, as much and as varied weaponry as they could lay their hands on in anticipation of a computer-induced apocalypse.

A small number of Christian evangelicals and fundamentalists believed that the Second Coming of Jesus Christ had to occur in AD 2000, and were looking for signs of the Last Days, the End Times as prophesied in various books of the Old and New Testaments, including Matthew, Daniel, Ezekiel and especially Revelation. Upheaval related to the Y2K bug and the Y2K bug itself were sure signs of the Tribulation. And a tiny minority of far-right evangelical Christian wingnuts turned openly hostile to federal government and what they perceived to be a Jewish conspiracy to thwart or oppose the dominion of God and his returning Son, Jesus Christ, and to somehow resist giving these wingnuts, armed to the teeth, of course, whatever it was the millennium was to bring them.

And if all this didn't get us, then misfiring intercontinental ballistic missiles would be chucking thermonuclear warheads all over the place and the whole place was set for, you know, KABLAMO!

Back in reality, there were governmental pleas for shared information and coordinated crisis-management efforts that went mostly unheeded. An International Y2K Cooperation Center was established in Washington, D.C., again by

President Clinton. Back over on this side of the Atlantic, apparently trying to soothe and reassure the public, the government of the United Kingdom intimated that, as in 1939, we would Keep Calm and Carry On, that we were fully prepared for all eventualities and that, thank God, the armed forces would provide assistance to local police if utilities, transportation systems or emergency services failed. They didn't say whether this preparation involved training on subjugation by force of the general and likely gone-mad citizenry, shoot-to-kill-on-sight policies, et cetera.

We should have known. After all, hadn't Eddie-from-*Friends*-lookalike Perry Farrell, kooky singer for dingbat Los Angelenos alt rockers Porno for Pyros, warned us from the main stage of the mud-fest quagmire of Woodstock in 1994 during an extended longueur of spoken-word free-associa-tion lunacy in the middle of their apocalypse/extinction/whatever-themed singalong hit 'Pets', that the millennium would be when the space aliens would introduce themselves to us. You know, because... crop circles and shit.

Meanwhile, I had started at Molextrics on the Monday morning after the presentation, the 5th of October 1998. A person who was introduced by a reception person as 'Mr Mole's Number 6' – a name followed, but I didn't catch it – took me deeper into the building and outlined what I would be doing... up to the end of the world – ha! – no, seriously, she said, what you'll be doing up to the millennium.

I was to work independently, though I would be 'integrating and interfacing' with the Networking, Product and Integration team. It became apparent this was three separate teams: there didn't seem to be an Interfacing team, and it wasn't made clear to me why I would not also be networking and producing anything with the teams that there were. I was given an office to myself high in the building.

Number 6 dropped me in there and said I would be 'hooked up' very soon, with a computer and telephone, I assumed. I was to focus solely on the problems that the Y2K bug would cause Mole's own networks and products. So mibby their integration was already identified as being impervious to shocks from the tick over from 1999 to 2000. And I supposed interfacing was just a tool of communication within the company and not something that needed any fixing in terms of how people interface with Mole networks or products, eh? 6 said something to the effect of, Sorry, you've lost me – 'you' being me and 'me' being 6, in this way of telling it. I said that nothing I was saying was of any consequence at the moment, I was just nervous, first day and all that, and tended to babble when I was nervous, twisting words and ideas round in my hands, mouth, brain, like I was nervously twisting a handkerchief in my hands. What are you saying? A handkerchief? 6 asked, as though such a thing was an unknown unknown. What age was 6? Everyone in the building so far seemed about 20. You know, I said, going for making it a known unknown if not a known known for 6, a thing for blowing and wiping your nose.

Oh, said 6, a tissue!

Yes, I capitulated, sighing.

After a silent second or two, and with a nod, 6 was gone and I saw no option but to sit on the pretty comfortable, full-ergonomic-features chair and stare for a while at the highly polished surface of my desk until the computer and telephone showed up, and mibby even the Networking, Product and Integration people arrived and did something unto me. Well, there was another option: going looking for a canteen, café, pool table and table tennis area if it was that kind of workplace, but 6 hadn't pointed out anything like that to me as we made our way deep into the building, and random wandering and random door pushing or pulling didn't appeal to me.

After a while of this waiting, and with each of the ergonomic features of the chair experimented with and settled, height, depth, incline, I stood at the window and looked out on Edinburgh. There was a good view across the New Town, and I was high up enough to be able to see down to the mad gothic of the Scott Monument. It was a view that I was going to become increasingly familiar with over the next year, in so far as I spent a lot of time staring out of that window, working my way through a number of problems. It was almost all head work. There was very little to do in a practical sense, in practical terms. I wouldn't be like Mr Scott going up that tube which he always had to do when technical and engineering things were most dire for the *Enterprise*, but not dire because of the dilithium crystal no being able to take much more. Whether the networks and products of Molextrics were actually going to fail at midnight on the 31st of December/1st of January had to be figured out in the abstract, not by, say, observation of the networks and products as they operated up to midnight. I thought about getting a whiteboard in the office. It seemed the kind of theoretical physicist or mathematician thing to do. But I didn't do this for a few months, until about the time I started suspecting that the Mole people started suspecting I wasn't doing anything at all. But let's not get ahead of ourselves.

After the first few days, and the arrival of my office infrastructure, a state-of-the-art, brand-new Viglen – Mole knew Sugar and they had some sort of agreement that Molextrics wasn't moving into computer-hardware manufacture and Sugar would keep his nose out of most other electronic products, or something like that, though Sugar was hoovering up contracts for computer supply to government, universities and private companies alike anyway – and a phone that looked like something out of the eighties with a set of speed dials that had been scrubbed over as the needs of the speed dialler had changed.

The next day an engineer of some sort, a software engineer – is this the correct term? a person from IT, anyway – arrived mid-morning to set up my access to all Molextrics networks, and also to set up my e-mail address. E-mail address? You have had one before, I take it, said the engineer/IT person/whatever. Oh yes, I said, since 1988. This was a half-lie. I had first seen the operation of an e-mail system – a USENET newsgroup – in about 1987, 1988, and I did have an e-mail address of my own after this, during my PhD – skduf98uhw*Y@meme.ed.ac.uk – but unusually for someone in that department at that time, I wasn't that into electronic mail, connectivity, networks. I had moved by then to being what was in essence a cultural critic, coming at everything from a sociological aspect. And anyway, I could never remember what my e-mail address was. The one I have given above is only an estimation of what it actually was. I mean, the @meme.ed.ac.uk I am fairly certain is correct, but all I remember about the bit before that, the bit where our names come these days, was just some set of letters, numbers and symbols and punctuation marks. The ICT people in the department had developed an office culture where they were more obsessed with security than interested in facilitated communication, so the system was both internal only, hence of limited use, and hence the use of the data-protection-conscious apparently randomised, and therefore incomprehensible, purposefully meaningless and therefore memory-evading jumble of letters, numbers, punctuation and symbols, which they insisted on changing once a month, furthering memory evasion.

The engineer brought up the account set up for me, a.a.strang@molextrics.co.uk. I felt a palpable sense of relief that this was, for the most part, comprehensible, though obviously I asked what the two As were for.

I suppose for your first and middle name, he said.

I don't have a middle name, I said.

Huh, he said. I dinnae ken, then, like.

Is it because my first name has more than one a?

I suppose so, aye, he said.

A couple of days after this, the first meeting with the heads of Networking, Product and Integration took place. They had all been at my presentation, I realised, but they carried themselves with such lack of gravitas I could have mistaken them for new starters. They all seemed to be in their twenties, too. I listened carefully to their concerns. The bottom line was that the Head of Networking was concerned about the networks, the Head of Product was concerned about the products and the Head of Integration was concerned that there was insufficient interfacing going on. I asked, Are you sure you don't mean 'integration'? She said quite distinctly, enunciating laboriously, No, *interfacing*. I nodded. All were concerned that the whole world was about to grind to a halt at the millennium because of the millennium bug. Because of Patrick I wasn't listening very carefully.

Well, I said, that's why I'm here.

Mole thinks you're a visionary, the Head of Product said.

Yes, he's been very nice about my abilities.

After a few months I told Mole himself that I couldn't work most effectively with just the crappy Viglen desktop they had provided me, and that to be most effective I needed a Thinkpad TF760XL laptop at the unthinkable expense of £3,855.00.

I explained to Mole and some top execs, plus the heads of departments, that I would be running a battery of tests during the time period from Christmas 1998 into the first few days of New Year 1999. I would be working through processes and procedures that would give us an intimate knowledge of what we would have to do — I would have to do — in the run-up to the millennium. I demanded that for full concentration on this task I needed to work alone, and it would be an idea to shut down the rest of Molextrics for this whole period. Well, since Christmas Day fell on a Friday in 1998, moving the Boxing Day bank holiday to the Monday, as well as New Year's Eve, which meant a bank holiday in Scotland on Monday the 4th of January because of the 2nd falling on a Saturday, it was easy enough to persuade a complete shutdown of the head office from end of play Christmas Eve to the 5th of January. A complete shutdown except for me working, that was. No one wanted to come in for three miserable days between Christmas and Hogmanay. In the ensuing chatter everyone seemed to suddenly be planning a getaway break with their families. Mole was in the Caribbean already, as was his annual routine, and I was explaining all this in the boardroom to people face to face except for Mole, who was coming through, *Charlie's Angels*-style, on a speaker phone.

So I would get what I wanted them to know I wanted, me alone with the full computing power of the whole Molextrics networks, and access to every working part of those networks so that I could, I told them, work through every last nook and cranny and test it to destruction.

Destruction? Mole's disembodied voice suddenly called.

The room went deathly silent.

Well, I said, You know, test it to the very limit of its, eh, limits. Ha! I'm not actually planning on des*troying* anything... obviously.

A ripple of laughter.

41

Aye, said Mole's voice. Mak sure ye dinnae, likesay, he said, employing that Scots technique of requiring dialect and accent to express something that was *pithily* the case.

Another ripple of laughter. The meeting broke up with pats on the back – on my back and sometimes between my colleagues – which somewhat mystified me, or mibby they were just congratulating me and each other on this nice wee long holiday break that had dropped from the sky, and invocations along the lines of, Nae des*troying*! Waggled fingers and the like. Dinnae be des*tructing*! All that kind of thing.

I made my preparations for the period of time I was going to be in work, concentrating hard on my work. I wanted as few and as little distractions as I could muster. If Y2K was a problem on a global scale, it was obvious to me and to everyone around me at Molextrics that a global-sized effort would be required. And I had taken it on single-handedly! What sacrifice! What martyrdom! I was like some insane saint, laying down my life that others will go on… be saved… I was like Jesus! The old Jesus complex, the old Crucifixion complex! Like those famous artists, whatshername and whatshisname. I read somewhere she was trying to paint him in a Crucifixion scene. Couple of nutters.

I got the food I needed in my house and in the office to minimise engagement with that, shut off all contact with any holiday break activities or communications and basically shut myself into a bubble that was only what I was doing, what I was thinking, what I was sensing and what this doing and thinking and sensing was telling me. Oh, and I meant to say, this was also about the time when, one morning, a few weeks before this, I woke up early, pre-dawn, and I don't mean woke up stretchy, yawny, half-asleep awake, I mean PING awake, feeling more awake than I ever had before, like I had spent my life up until this moment, this *second*, half asleep, asleep when awake and just more deeply asleep when asleep, and as I lay there awake into the dawn, watching the objects in my eyeline – I daren't move lest I became even *more* awake, hyperawake – solidify as they resolved in the dawn light, it seemed every hair on my head was alive to the present I was in, and my brain was alive to everything in the past. I was remembering every moment of the past year or so, as my heart thudded dully down there under the quilt. Of course, there were individual salient memories, that time this, this time that, scenes rose up, came towards me, played out, but they were just the frothing white tops of a wave of an ocean of so many precise memories of the past year, a tsunami of *all* the memories of the last year, and, like the rising water of a tsunami, it came in, hit, swamped me, carried me inland in its wake, if wake is the right word, for a mile or two, subsided, went out and left me strewn in a tree, clinging to a branch. It took me ages to get back to sleep, and that was just the start of a long period of time when I wasn't half asleep any more. I was awake. I barely slept at all during this time.

When the rest of the staff returned to the office on the 5th, the devastation was absolute and immediately obvious. Mole, execs, board members, heads of departments all crowded at the door of my office and my equipment was in… pieces. Plastic casing and metal wiring scrap, a motherboard snapped in two. Two large CRT monitors I had set up on the desk were now both smashed through with repeated heavy, crashing kicks and lay on the floor on their sides. It was eight o'clock in the morning and I looked as though I hadn't slept, gone home, washed or engaged in any normal human activities in forty-eight, mibby seventy-two hours.

The testing… went OK, then? Mole said. He could be funny when he wanted to be. This is, I hope, all that got des*troyed*?

43

I can't work with these, I said, kicking one of the CRT screens. Then, unpredictably, even to myself, I screamed, CATHODE-RAY TUBES, FOR CHRIST'S SAKE, IS TECHNOLOGY INVENTED IN THE LAST CENTURY!

It's not the next century yet, one of the younger execs said.

Mole turned to her. He actually means the last century, he said. Cathode-ray technology was invented in the 1890s.

Really? came the answer.

Really, Mole said.

All this equipment is just… SHIT, I said, again unpredictably emotional about the situation.

I think perhaps leaving you to this, alone, was not quite the sparkling idea it seemed, Mole said.

I had been looking down at the CRT monitors, and I looked up and said, YEAH. I mean, I just can't – Mole! How WAS your HOLIDAY in the *Caribbean*? Where is it you *actually* GO, anyway? I heard you *own an island* or something, have a *big* place out *THERE*. I sounded absolutely crazed. I couldn't regulate the tone, pitch or volume of my voice at all.

I think you need some time to come back to us, Mole said, and he swept his arm around the little crowd around him, all of whom, except the person who was always at Mole's side, sort of dissolved from view. Really, he said, how did the testing go?

Oh, that, I said. Fine. Actually *absolutely* fine. It's just the TOOLS at my disposal…

Yes, I see, Mole said.

THIS IS WINDOWS 95, FOR CHRIST'S SAKE!

I'll expect a new quote for kit.

Yes. Yes. Yes. I'll get that to you, I said.

I think we need to get you some support.

Support?

People.

NO! I mean, no. You're worrying too much. This...
I indicated the smashed equipment. That was just...
frustration. I'm identifying and solving so many... things.
My concentration is geared *up*, I'm *fully* focused. People
would only be a distraction.

Two colleagues were looking at each other. I thought I saw
one nod, side-eyeing, then the other did the same. I think.
Whatever.

As long as you're sure.

I AM. I... am. The equipment was just bothering me. With
the equipment I need... I'll need new equipment, obviously.
But with it I can make even greater progress... quicker.

Well, OK, Mole said.

Just be ready when I identify what I need.

Take a break – at least do that for me. A couple of days,
at least.

Yeah.

At least.

Yeah. I hear you.

So I told Mole's IT people, as it was best to keep Mole
himself out of it, that I actually needed more memory, an
unimaginably huge 5GB, that could only be achieved by
purchase of a Gateway Solo 9100 S5-233XL – it always had
to be XL – that I needed more computing firepower if I was
going to get anywhere. £4,228.00. A note came from Mole
which read:

BUT WE'VE ONY JUST SPENT 4 GRAND A FEW
MOTHS AGO!

His consistent uppercase had a curiously childlike aspect.
His misspelling of ONLY and MONTHS seems to speak
for itself, though I don't think people who can't spell are
lesser intellects, and I don't think writing in consistent
uppercase helps. In fact, what seems most peculiar now is

that it was handwritten at all. Why hadn't he written me an e-mail, or at least word processed and printed out the note?

There were luddites about, I suppose. These really were still pretty primitive times for computing, e-mails, networking, all that, that we were living in. You could see how everything was going to change, and how rapid that change would be, even as we lived through it. And old ways of working, they're so powerful, aren't they? I saw one of the administrators at Molextrics who had been with the company for many years, and he just could not handle not having his word processing pushed to print immediately. And this habit had been dragged through using an electronic typewriter into the computer era. He still used Tipp-Ex, for Christ's sake! Can you imagine?

It was during these months up to the millennium that people started making more serious plans about how they were going to spend it. Simultaneously the feeling among colleagues that I was a spare part seemed to dissipate as fear that the world was going to grind to a halt on millennium night started to take serious grip. I don't think they suddenly started thinking I was some kind of visionary genius who was about to avert their apocalypse. Most seemed convinced, because I had so comprehensively dodged every presentation on what I had been doing for them and the company, that I was at best hopeless and at worst secretive. A few started speaking to me in a strangely literal way, with very direct declarative statements, avoiding all aspects of the language of emotion and feelings.

It all started because I have this vice I have of creating a bit of thinking time by repeating the last word or phrase someone says to me before responding.

One day a colleague said to me, How's the work going?

And I replied, Going? How's it going?

I mean, how is it coming along?

Coming along? I repeated.

Now the colleague was getting a wee bit flustered and I was kind of enjoying this.

I mean. Let me start again. What progress have you made in the task of ensuring that the Y2K does not adversely affect Molextrics?

I couldn't see how I could repeat any of that mouthful, so I capitulated. Ah! I said. Yes, some progress. I don't like estimating…

No, no, my colleague said.

But I can say fifty per cent. I had the kind of impression he wanted an exact figure. Fifty-one per cent, I said, and smiled.

That sounds promising. You must be starting to have a good feeling.

Feeling? I repeated.

After this conversation I've just described, the colleague I was talking to and a couple of others started enunciating very distinctly whenever they were speaking to me, and slowly, though not in a patronising way, but as though they were thinking through every single word they were about to say. More like someone with a heavy dialect or accent trying to be understood when way outside their accent or dialect comfort zone. But they did sound kind of mad. I started thinking they were autistic in some way that I had not noticed previously, until the inevitable overhearing of a conversation that made it clear, confirmation as though confirmation were needed, that they thought I was autistic, and they were trying to improve the way they communicated with me so as to draw out of me… I'm not exactly sure what. What I was doing, I guess.

But they can't work in groups, on group work, I heard one opine. They get pissed off with group work. They feel people, colleagues, other people, just get in their way. They're focused on the task, on the machine, the software, the network.

Where are you getting this from? You seem well versed in what autistic people are supposed to be like, the other person said.

Well, there's an online page of facts and myths these days. National Autistic Society.

Yeah, there's a web page for everything these days, I suppose. All campaigning groups and charities. Newest way of advertising themselves.

They're all getting people, Web Consultants. If you don't have an online strategy you're dead in the water.

That's when I decided to continue my way into the coffee room. What are you guys saying? I asked. Web consultants?

They jumped, wondering when I had been able to hear from.

We were just saying, one of them said, that an interesting phenomenon is the rise of online strategies for businesses, charities. They have to have webpages, or you see 'webpage under construction' all over the Internet.

Interesting? I said, playing along.

Um, engaging? Necessary? I... he looked to his colleague.

Eh... I suppose... There's money to be made?

Lucrative, I said, as affectless as I could manage.

Yes! That's it, lucrative.

The other colleague was nodding. They were relieved to have got to a concrete-enough concept for me.

Yes, I think web consultancy might be something I'll look at after I finish on this Y2K work. Maybe the one you mentioned will be needing help.

The one I mentioned?

Yes, I said. National Autistic Society, was it?

Yes, yes, it was.

There was a general fluster of activity, and my colleagues were making their way out of the room.

Yeah, I feel quite good about that prospect, I said, just to give them a confusing kiss-off.

About this time I repeated to the IT people that the real problem was not the computing firepower, but the Windows 95 operating system. I went on to tell them that I could get more done, and more quickly, with an Apple Powerbook 3400C/240. And I want Apple's newly developed LCD displays, three of them, as large as they come, I said.

Apple? How can that possibly make sense? some IT geek asked me on the phone: it was best not to confront them face to face, I had found.

It was the CRT displays that sent me over the edge, I said. By this time everyone knew I was an emotionally unstable wreck doing what I was doing on the Y2K bug. I was Sisyphus.

He won't like it, IT said.

But I had broken Mole by this stage. The agreement for a further £4,346.00 for the laptop alone came from him without comment. I don't exactly know how much the three LCD displays were, but I think I was paying off about half of Apple's R&D costs for having developed them.

It was also during the weeks and months up to the millennium that you started to hear people talking about their feelings about the millennium and, more specifically, what their plans were for millennium night. Mostly this was a fairly bog-standard set of comments like, We're going to my mother's, I'm spending it with my sister's family, We've hired a cottage in Aberfoyle, We'll just hunker down at home, I don't like Hogmanay and just go to bed, You have to go big on Hogmanay, of course, so we'll be out and about in Edinburgh and'll probably end up watching the fireworks,

I'll get plastered, and all the rest. But then there were little intimations of ideas that this Hogmanay and New Year was something to be apprehensive about – to fear, even. We're stocking up on everything, seemed to be a common theme in this strain of response. When I said, Stocking up? I got the answer, Well, we always stock up for New Year anyway, with the shops being shut through to the… At this point, quite a few people would pause and realise or check that the 31st fell on Friday, meaning that the 1st would be a Saturday, the second a Sunday, negating these as bank holidays, with the 3rd and 4th therefore being the bank holidays for Scotland.

Do you think that means shops will be shut from the Friday to the Wednesday? people would ask in almost shocked disbelief. Then they would play a game of negotiation about the size of shops, the square footage and the size of any chain that they were part of, the proximity of this or that shop to their homes, the recent and sometimes ancient history of this shop's shutting or otherwise on public holidays, the possibility of the new Scottish Parliament or some other executive function of the state – local government, Westminster – might abrogate this hiatus in civil functioning or at least its length by moving one or both bank holidays to be scattered at more opportune moments through the rest of the year 2000. What was for sure was that someone somewhere had better do something about this! A society cannot be suspended just like that for four whole days! Even without some collapse due to the Millennium Bug, this was a step too far! What were we all supposed to do with ourselves? For *four days*? With no shops, cinema, cafés? This is when the Exocet missile would hit the brain and a tremulous voice would pipe up:

My God, you don't think the *pubs* are going to be shut that whole time? Then a little plead: Do you?

This was Armageddon field enough for some folks, and a Sodom and Gomorrah of the soul would stalk the land. What would people *get up to* in this dark land of being left to their own devices, shut up in their own houses, for four days? And potentially with relatives! Bloody blue murder would be general! Screaming into the night would be routine! Drug taking legal and illegal of any and all sorts would be necessary. Barbarism! Sawney Beanism! An end to civilisation!

Obviously by this point in their thinking many were making plans to be out of the country or as far from towns and cities as they could make by plane, train, ferry, bus, car or even, if need be, by pushbike or on foot.

Aaaaaaaaaaaaaaaaaaaaargh! It really did feel like *run for your life* time. The Millennium Bug? SO WHAT? The situation was already dire!

Idiots. As though you couldn't get an extra this and one more of that until the shops opened again on the Wednesday? Jesus Christ. And a shut-out from the pub could possibly do you good, dry out a bit, as long as you didn't get too much extra booze in the house. Though mibby I was just thinking of my own personal circumstances over these days, which were looking distinctly cosy and pleasant, a chance to chill out and relax, listen to music, watch some telly and veg, with people I liked and loved. I know you shouldn't just think that if you'll be OK then everyone can set themselves up to be OK too, but, come on. If you hate your in-laws or your oldest friend or whoever, no one says you cannot avoid them. Well, OK, people do say that, but it's not a law or anything!

6

15 days to go

OH FOR FUCK'S SAKE, WHY AM I LYING? Why am I fucking *lying*? God, I have to stop this. Stop all the bloody lies I have been telling. Stop, stop, stop, stop. I mean, the way I've told you this story is one way of telling you what I was doing in the months and weeks up to the millennium, but hardly the truth, the whole truth and nothing but the truth, so help me God.

For example, see all those laptops I demanded in succession? Well, I did demand them, that is true, but this is what happened. On one of the first days after I got set up with the Viglen desktop I started browsing around and scrolling through web pages on the Internet, which was pretty much a new experience for me. I mean, there were computers all around us when I was studying memetics, but I was actually working hard at getting my qualifications and just didn't have much time and, frankly, no inclination to spend my time idly browsing. The word itself has all the horror in it of 'browsing the shops', an activity I find horrific: when I shop I shop *for* something and then get the hell out of there; browsing in a bookshop is a little less horrific: a *little*. And when I then worked in advertising, selling memes to the masses, yes, there were computers all over the place there as well, usually Apple Macintosh Powerbooks and Power

Macs, but this was mostly for effect; sometimes people would play with fonts on them. But they were in essence nice lamps for the spaces – 'offices' seemed a dirty word. We worked in 'spaces', in 'studios', in 'workshops', 'breakout rooms', 'breakout spaces', or, worst of all, 'creative spaces', and we worked by 'brainstorming', by 'getting creative', by 'workshopping' – by, I suppose, 'breaking out'. None, or not much, of this involved browsing or scrolling. Mostly it was people sitting in small or large groups, with a spectrum from everyone sitting in essence in silence, thinking, to tumultuously arguing, shouting, and, in one case, a fistfight was what 'broke out'. Sorry, I'm becoming digressive, but that was also what was happening to me then. So, bored browsing the Internet on the Viglen, I went along to the room that had some easy chairs and a coffee percolator – how seventies! how retro! – and sat watching coffee percolate. Then I noticed on the coffee table in front of me a copy of *For Him Magazine*, *FHM*, one of these lads' mags that had tried to stretch the glossy magazine demographic into blokes, lads, men, with a few tasteful shots of lovely ladies, often celebrities, in their underwear, though strictly no more naked, and some articles on things, objects, items, gear, and, once in a while, relationships. Now, here was some old fashioned browsing I could do. I was a glossy-mag kind of person, after all. So I started flicking through pages and that's when I came to a page entitled 'On your knees!', a suitably blokeish way for a Paul Pettengale to introduce spending his time and effort as he 'picks out the smallest, smartest laptops' available in 1998. My point is, all my demands for laptops was just me picking my way down the list of laptops on this page, except for the two cheap, shit ones. So, I had been getting all my information from one *Which?*-like article in *FHM*. For some reason a lad's mag could make me seem like a technical genius. Who knew? The secret seemed to be to mention all the numbers and XLs after the make and model. In these times this is what qualified you for technical respect. Oh, and an RTFM tendency, including wearing the T-shirt, that I flannelled a few people with.

And LCD monitors. I only knew about them because of Patrick. And only because Patrick is an Apple-hater and said any second now LCD would be everywhere, universal, cheap and reliable, unlike Apple shit.

I was in the office a lot in the final countdown to the millennium. In our offices there was a Molextrics electronic clock, specially designed by Mole himself, which started a countdown at 2,678,400.000 seconds to midnight on Hogmanay/New Year's Day from midnight at the start of the 1st of December 1999. It sat in the foyer of the building, behind the reception desk, whirling downwards, at a rate of a thousandth of a second. As I arrived that morning, I remember distinctly the numbers that weren't blurred read 1261725 when I glanced at the clock. I read it as 126, 1725, which struck me because 1725 was the year that the astronomers James Bradley and Samuel Molyneux set up a telescope in Molyneux's observatory to observe the stellar parallax of Gamma Draconis, the brightest start in the constellation of Draco. It was this work that led to the discovery of the astronomical aberration of light, stellar aberration or velocity aberration, the phenomenon by which stars appear to shift about a bit when observed because the observer is also in motion, what with the earth rotating one revolution once a day and whizzing round the Sun once a year and the Sun whizzing round the Milky Way at whatever rate it does that, et cetera. And, of course, the stars are all whipping around the universe in their predictable and unpredictable ways as well.

I was thinking of all this as I glanced at the clock countdown and saw 1725, additionally, because, for some reason, the whole clock display blurred on this number, sparkled and wobbled. I remember thinking, That's like the aberration of light for the stars. Because I'm in motion passing the clock, the clock just seemed to wobble there for that number. And that's when it suddenly struck me that there was this thing in the networks, and in the products, this anomaly, a… gap, an aberration that, had we not considered the motion of the observer when observing the movement of time within the networks and products then, yes, just mibby, possibly, not probably but possibly, this glitch, this aberration could lead to a wholesale shutdown of all Molextrics networks and products. I rapidly dismissed the thought. I couldn't think it through to an end point, so it probably meant nothing at all.

And, anyway, were we to truly address this tiny gap, the gap I was thinking about, it really came down to the exact positioning of the earth at the exact time of 00.00.0000, midnight of the millennium. For that I needed accurate data from the Global Positioning System, the only long-developed and reliable way of knowing exactly where you are using satellites. But, from the Indo-Pakistani conflict in Kargil over the summer, we knew that United States government agencies had been deploying a Selective Availability policy that meant few people other than the United States government had access to such data. And even if they had given me access to it, the rumour was that at best they could estimate within five metres of where anything was at the exact time you needed to know, this having something to do with not enough satellites, not enough clear sight triangulation points.

I gave Patrick a call. I laid out my concerns in a rushed and incoherent way, no doubt, but it was clear enough what

I was suggesting to him. I said, finally, Is that something? Is that something you haven't considered? Is it something that means the bug could be actual, or virtual, virtual but actual, actually virtual?

I heard a sigh. Then he said, Nup. Then the sound of him ending the call.

Counterproductive and self-defeating, yes, but the only way to stay sane seemed to be to just suppress and forget what I had only just been thinking. I mean, Patrick, he was the expert, wasn't he? I walked through the foyer and up the stairs to my office, feeling curiously out of breath by the time I reached it. I needed more exercise, I thought to myself, to be breathless after so little exertion. As soon as I was done with this charade of a job I would take my money and take a holiday, a cycling or hill-walking holiday, just to get back into shape. Or mibby I would lie on a sun lounger for a month, and dips in the pool each morning would keep me as fit as I need be.

Again suddenly, my picturing of this sun-lounger scene disappeared and was replaced with my being thrown from the Mole building in disgrace, a collection of pathetic, meagre possessions in a box, with Mole in person screaming at me, YOU WON'T BE GETTING A PENNY, YOU *CHARLATAN*! It's daytime, morning, 7.00 A.M., and alarms from within the building are still going off from midnight, when the whole Molextrics network and every Molextrics product have simultaneously ground to a halt as 1999 has become 2000.

The truth is, this is what I've been doing during this whole time working for Molextrics.

One day, staring out the window down to the Scott Monument, and sort of thinking about old Sir Walter, wondering if there was writing of his I liked, or might like if I read it. He was an uber-privileged scion of a prominent

Edinburgh family and naturally, if these things can be natural, a Tory; an elitist; a solid, clubbable man; a Freemason. He was a romantic, that necessary if frowsy progression in thinking in Western cultures, which got us through to the scientific enlightenment of the 19th and 20th century. He admired the English progressive and reforming novelist Maria Edgeworth's representation of Irish life, but misinterpreted her works as an attempt to strengthen the Anglo-Irish Union, his own conviction more than hers. Perception of his underlying Scots nationalism is probably more looked for than there, and he basically invented Scots tourist tartan tattery in 1822 for the visit of King George IV to Edinburgh. A UK-wide banking crisis caused his financial ruin, which is hardly a reason to cry for a man, but no one would deny sympathy to a man who lost his wife at about the same time. He wanted to do for Scottish thinking and literature something like what had happened in German thinking and literature. But what was there about him that I could be sympathetic or empathetic to? What could I admire? He was an Edinburgh man through and through, despite his associations with London, specifically London society, and his family ties to the borders. He was a disabled man, affected by polio at a young age, though this in itself should not arouse our pity, and may be considered only a part of what maketh the man. In a sense, Scott was and is, with his monstrous monument dominating Edinburgh's premier shopping street and therefore the Route 1 of the nonsensical tourist trail, every bit as intricate and heavy and barren as his reputation, the very apex of a type of Caledonian Antisyzygy: he both brought Scotland, and especially the Highlands, to central consideration within European culture, while at the same time giving many aspects of it a down-his-nose comicality, marginality, clownishness. The kings and dukes were to be admired and lauded and the poor farmers and workers brought local comical colour and a laugh to the lips of the reader. And that's when this wholly unrelated idea popped into my head:

One day, God was going around, you know, being omnipotent, moving in a mysterious way and all that, when he fell into an existential crisis – God's second-biggest existential crisis after the I'M LONELY!!!!! *cri de cœur* of, you know, creating everything. He was thinking of miscarriage as a biological reality and inevitability of the way the human body is designed, and He realised, with the number of miscarriages that occur in the natural course of things for all animals and in the human population, which was particularly on His mind, them being made in His image and all, meant that He, the maker of all things, the prime mover, all that is, He was the greatest abortionist of all time. If the anti-abortionists were right that abortion was murder pure and simple, then He had murdered millions, billions, millions of billions. Would His worshippers forgive Him? Could He forgive Himself?

It was a curious little amusement, an obvious reversal joke, born out of a slight anger I felt listening to some self-described Fundamental Evangelical Christians on a street in the Old Town saying what they would like to do to doctors up to and including killing them, because life was sacrosanct in the womb, though obviously not after graduation from medical school. For a while I thought I could work this up into something. I wasn't quite sure what. A comedy routine, to perform at the Fringe, mibby? But was it funny?

This was the start of a series of pretty stray thoughts as I stared out of the window and down at the Scott Monument, when I wasn't imagining the Monument as Thunderbird 3 and taking off.

His second-biggest existential crisis? Ha. Fifteenth, mibby. Come on. Let's think this through. I mean, there was all sorts of existentialism going on when He was just sat there, outside time and space, twiddling His thumbs before the crisis of realising He could speak, because He wasn't speaking to, well, the nothingness, or at best Himself before coming up with the completely exasperated, Oh for God's sake! LET THERE BE LIGHT! Then there would have been the crisis of Him realising that if He said stuff it happened! That's got to be full of regret, that, hasn't it? Man, He must have been thinking, I shoulda done this bloody years ago! If, you know, years had existed back then, like, before I just created time. Then after He had got down to it, dividing the night from the day and the sea from the land and creating the beasts and the fowl and the things that swimmeth in the sea and crawleth upon the earth and all that jazz, coming up with a man and a woman, created in His own image, He must have felt that slight twinge that all who begat feel, that His time was partly up, that He had a replacement of sorts, He had, in a sense, a rival, He had been superseded, made obsolete, deposed. He had set another wheel in motion – though He perhaps put it a wee bit differently, as all this creation business didn't seem to account for mere historical things like the invention of the wheel – and now the world was the world of the man and woman. And then He got, before everyone else – He wasn't stupid, God – to the existential crisis of, if He was creating everything, who created Him? Perhaps that's when He hit the existential crisis that left Him up in His bedroom in heaven all day and all night, moping, even though it was a lovely sunny day outside and everyone else was going for a picnic, up there with His curtains closed, and that bloody racket music going, reading that doom-laden stuff, Dostoevsky or Camus or Nietzsche – women need not apply – with the dawning realisation that smiting sounded good, nice work if He could get it. And the hair and the eyeliner and the clothes after Him reading Nietzsche. God Almighty! And Him on and on about how He felt dead, dead on the inside, dead on the outside.

The God scenario, either the abortion one or the God existential crisis teenager one I had just been thinking through, could be a short story that I would develop and make both funnier and more searingly angry, I thought.

Each one would have a little smack of what the God as abortionist story had.

As I started naming the short stories of a collection I was going to call *My Book of Revelations*, warming to a theme of how the millennium was unlikely to be the apocalypse, or no more the apocalypse than all previous apocalypses, I came up with a manipulation of the title of the 1951 science fiction classic, *The Day the Earth Stood Still*. I did the easy swap:

The Day the Earth Still Stood

See what I did there? Next title I got is a manipulation of the Joan Didion essay 'On the Morning after the Sixties', but I didn't know this until I looked it up a moment ago. I knew the title of the song 'The Morning after the Sixties' by the Leeds punk/dance band Age of Chance that I heard on a John Peel Session from 1985. My story was about the millennium, or was going to be, once I wrote it, so my title had to be,

The Morning after the Nineties

I was starting to think there was a relationship between the ideas I was having for these stories. I could see the first two would relate to each other, at least. It would be about parties and the end of parties as 1999 became 2000. Next title I got was:

Far from the Mad In-Crowd

A pretty smart wordplay on the title of Hardy's fourth novel, *Far from the Madding Crowd*, I thought. These were going OK. I was getting somewhere with them. The book would be about an escape away from some smart set, about the better party to be had if we all just dropped our delusions. The days around a millennium party in Edinburgh, but among the hoi polloi.

At one point, moving the action to a setting I was more familiar with, Glasgow, and thinking about the sometimes aggressive inhospitality and general putdownness and putdownability of the people of Glasgow, who would put down even their loved ones if they were perceived to be rising above their station, which I felt, in a moment of negativity about my city, which I was at liberty to have complex feelings about as it was mine,

There Is No 'There, There' There

Which you'll know, being an intelligent and well-read person, *sans doute*, is a playful rewrite of Gertrude Stein's famous statement about the place, or lack of place, she came from – Oakland, California: 'there is no there there'. Vague scenes and ways of writing these stories came to me, fitfully, then desultorily, and then I'd return to reordering the list of chapter titles I had.

I got my next title, every story still just being a title for a story, or for these interrelated stories, which, I suppose, could also be considered chapters, from Kirk Douglas's movie about Van Gogh, *The Agony and the Ecstasy*. If you knew your nineties in the UK, or America, or mibby all over the world, about partying all over the world, this just had to be,

The Ecstasy and the Agony

Though I couldn't quite see how the agony bit was going to come in. I hate 'My Drug Hell' stories. I'm not saying people don't descend into these, and I'm not saying I look down at people who do as weak or stupid. I just am mostly bored by them. It's like drug taking and consequences as apocalypse, when the truth is most people take most drugs, have an OK time, then it's back to work, or school, or back on duty. It was just tabloid to think one spliff, two weeks later mainlining H, one week later death. Come on. Garbage. It all says so much more about the requirements of a story – character, plot, drama, jeopardy – than it did about reality. It made me think about all the pop-culture detritus that lies around everywhere in our lives and how it's all OK really, which led to a quick and easy reversal from the title of Blur's 1993 album *Modern Life Is Rubbish* to the more life-affirming,

Modern Rubbish *Is* Life

Mibby it was the Blur connection, but I suddenly was resiting these stories to a London setting as mibby I was still more convinced of the London primacy in all things New Yearish, and with Joan Didion still in mind, when I did a rewrite on the title of the 'Swinging London' documentary from 1967, *Tonite Let's All Make Love in London*. But I mashed this together with the hyperconsumerism of our own *No Logo*ed age,

Tonite Let's All Love Makes in London

I could see now clearly, this was a novel, with whip-smart chapter titles. I was feeling pretty pleased with myself. The chapters would only need writing now. It seemed like anything that came to mind – like the 1969 film of Horace 'Mack' McCoy's Depression-era dancethon book *They Shoot Horses, Don't They?*, which to my mind seemed to chime with the E'd-up youth ravers coming down – could be repurposed, in this case into:

They Don't Shoot Horses, Do They?

I wanted a big finishing chapter, something schlocky and horrifying, a version of the Scottish play ending, mibby, where everyone dies, and I stuck together every schlock horror title word I could think of and came up with:

Revenge Attack of the 50 ft Monster Teenage Kung Fu Killer Zombie Mega-Vixens from *Beyond* Planet Mutoid in Outer Space... 2

I thought it had a nice rounding off from the first chapter. It was quite clear these were chapter titles of a novel, still to be called *My Book of Revelations*. How long did I work on this? How many hours? And how far past the chapter titles did I get? you might ask. Well, I made a list of them. I rearranged them a number of times. I thought about what they might contain, stories of this, and of that, all centred around the millennium.

One night, a rare night off at the time, I was back home watching Channel 4. This was at the time that *Frasier* was one of the most popular – if not the most popular – shows on the channel: on the 1st January 1999, for example, the channel had broadcast a *Frasier* Night dedicated to the show, with behind-the-scenes documentaries and star interviews. It wasn't that night I'm talking about, though, just a usual night of *Frasier* being on. I watched as the whip-smart title cards came up for the sections of the show. You know the sort of thing, 'Kentucky Freud Chicken', 'Roz Is a Roz Is a Roz Is a Roz', 'The Jungian and the Restless', that sort of thing. I mean, I had seen this before, but not really noticed what form they took, nor how much my own little wordplay chapter titles resembled these title cards.

It was like one of those anticipated intercontinental ballistic missiles, a small one, had just hit and blasted right through me, and I imagined myself like one of those cartoon characters, hilariously mutilated, with a ragged circle hole punched clean through my torso, and the animator depicts a heart and lungs and lower abdomen and other organs still kind of working away, with me still alive and standing, a look more of surprise than horror on my face. I felt that destroyed. I could hear that sad and pitiful not-funny-at-all *mwap mwap mwaah* sound that seemed to fit perfectly with the visual joke.

I knew I hadn't and wasn't just lying to my colleagues, wasting their time and defrauding Mole of money, I had actually lied to myself and wasted my time and I wasn't just defrauding people, I was myself a fraud. I was so smart, wasn't I? Fooling everyone. But the thing is I do mean everyone, myself included. Thoughts died from my mind. The novel dropped dead with this as well. I was probably never going to write it anyway. What kind of writer was I, anyway? No kind of writer at all. I had just unconsciously picked up a wordplay habit from a popular show and thought I was creating something. I wasn't creating something. I was creating nothing. Just repeating a joke I had heard. This left me feeling bleak indeed. There was no longer any impetus for this kind of writing.

There would be no *My Book of Revelations* – not in the way I then conceived it, anyway.

That was about the time the sleeping thing kicked in. Who knows what this was about. Boredom, mibby. Or proof I was actually working really hard on *something*, just not anything to do with what I was being contracted to do. Or mibby it was depression. Nah, it wasn't depression. Could it have been depression? Just feeling sleepy all the time?

The first time I was found asleep in my chair, sitting up though slightly slumped, I put it down to an all-nighter I had pulled that the CCTV in the building's corridors and public spaces would have quickly proved didn't happen. I had left late, as was usual, but had arrived early, as was unusual, which let my story hold water unless someone wanted to check it out thoroughly.

The second time, Mole himself found me semi-slumped in front of my screens and I kept it simpler. I just said I was knackered, this was a tiring business. I don't know why he took this at face value. Something to do with the countdown nature of my task, the belief that we Y2K engineers were working both around the clock and against the clock, let any behaviour be seen in this light. He nodded pityingly and wandered away. Probably off on his fifteenth holiday in the Caribbean this year. I heard his place out there was some family thing – he didn't come from nothing after all; his people had or had had money.

The fourteenth or fifteenth time I was caught asleep at the wheel, as it were, I was simply woken by an office cleaner, who seemed to be trying to vacuum the carpet below me and wanted me to, exasperated-mother-and-teenage-lazybones style, lift my feet and legs out of the way.

People had started to seem as though they expected me to be asleep in my office more often than awake. It all just proved how insanely hard I was working, was the thinking. Mibby they thought I was still working when asleep, literally trying to dream up the solution to these myriad Y2K problems.

When I stopped with this fanciful thinking about suddenly becoming a writer, I realised what I actually had on my hands was a meme. God the abortionist. Linking it with the wholly natural process of miscarriage. It was a little thought bomb. As a memeticist, of course this is what I had come up with.

What I really wanted to invent, to create, though, was a process meme, a tiny thought that people would incorporate into their belief system. That's when I came up with the e-mail meme, the substance of which was that I would communicate, disseminate, distribute the idea – how I wasn't quite sure – that I or someone had developed a piece of software that would allow a receiver of an e-mail to be able to use a kind of undo typing button on any e-mail sent to them, wheeling back through previous edits made to the e-mail. Once this thought had taken, I thought, then every last person who had ever written that angry, swearing, ranting draft before delete delete delete and drafting the frustratingly diplomatic and bland e-mail they eventually sent would be like, Oh-oh. I also got a laugh out of the idea of people peering at their e-mail interface, searching, searching for this magical undo-typing button.

I was in my office looking out of the window, quite reasonably saying to myself that this was just my mind racing away with me, or from me, that the likelihood of the said aberration… the glitch… anomaly… the, um, the… um, er, the um… Was the Scott Monument wobbling? Was Edinburgh wobbling? Was the world wobbling, more than on its axis, as it does, imperceptibly, but perceptibly wobbling, here, now, before my eyes?

I went through to a small windowless staff room we had just along the corridor.

Four or five people in here.

The kettle, I was staring at the kettle, because I couldn't look… at them.

The effect had begun in my eyes. I thought, Am I excited? Am I about to jump up? Run? Was I going to punch…

something. The wall? Someone. Jennifer? Then it came to me. I was alarmed. But I don't mean that in the usual way, in the usual usage of the word. I was alarmed in the way a vehicle is alarmed, like a bank is alarmed, a jeweller's, the Molextrics building. Like a nuclear power station is alarmed. And the alarms were about to go off. Were I to… smoke a cigarette, drink some water, drink a glass of vodka, a bottle of wine, a bottle of vodka, take a drug to calm me down. I took Lorazepam for a muscle thing once. 2 mg. 5 mg. 50 mg. Something. If I were to tear my hair out. Be put to sleep for days. Induced coma.

I was looking around myself, at the people, and at Jennifer, who was coming towards me.

It seemed to be something to do with the nystagmus in my eyes as they wobbled and the way I now could not catch a breath, but the people around me stopped being themselves. I perceived them, as best I could perceive them at all, as shell simulacra of the people they were. It was not Jennifer that I saw talking to me, but a thin shell version of her, like she was one of those moulded plastic lamps in the shape of Mickey Mouse or Snoopy or some such, empty but for a bulb and a fitting with a wire to the plug, which is plugged into a socket. And I was faintly surprised that Jennifer wasn't just coming clean about her new status as an empty shell person. Why wouldn't she accept and note this new state of affairs? I mean, it's not as though she was lit up like she would be were she actually one of these lamps. And she was animate, could move her limbs and lips, and she was talking to me and gesticulating.

But it was just so obvious that she wasn't the person I knew as Jennifer, the one with skin and muscle and nerves and bones and internal organs. This doppelganger in front of me was more of a thing, an object, than a person. Whether some transformation had taken place in Jennifer and this was her now transformed, or whether Jennifer, the person-Jennifer, was elsewhere and this animate object shell version of her was also in the world, going about Jennifer-like activities, talking to me in a Jennifer-like way, was unclear. I suppose that one could only be cleared up if the person-Jennifer also arrived on the scene while shell-Jennifer was still here. She continued to talk to me.

And I said I 'perceived' a moment ago, but this isn't quite right. Because I did know, or felt fairly sure, that Jennifer and the other people around me were these shell simulacra, but I didn't know this from looking at them and listening to them. Well, I mean, yes, it was because of the way they looked and sounded and presented themselves that I knew they were what I thought they were, but the thing is that they were exact replicas of who they were, or who they had been. I knew, felt fairly sure, they were empty, and empty of human qualities, of physical qualities of being a human, but they were simply known to me by their nature. I couldn't technically perceive their nature because of the imperceptibility of any difference whatsoever between their human form and this.

I started to feel disconcerted. And then all the alarms went off: the siren; the flashing red lights; the screeching bleep; the wail; the flashing text:

DANGER, DANGER, DANGER,
CRITICAL TEMPERATURE REACHED;

the verbal alarm:

WARNING, WARNING,
MAKE YOUR WAY OUTSIDE;

the vibration beneath my feet, a deaf-blind person's alarm. And I noticed every time Jennifer talked to me, I was holding my breath, waiting for this absurd pantomime to fall to pieces and the shell to break apart and crumble to the floor. But she wasn't. Somehow she held together, fragile – I just knew she was fragile, she didn't look or sound fragile – as she was.

Then, when Jennifer turned to one of the other simulacra to comment on this or that – a few of them had gathered close to us – I knew that actually what was being communicated between them was that they were this new kind of thing, this new kind of being that was all shell and no old-fashioned lungs and heart and bone and muscle and skin and eyes, like I was, and that they were really communicating that they all knew this about me and were laughing with each other about my left-behind status as an old-style person that had not made the transition or been replaced with the shiny shell existence: I realised they did look shiny, though in exactly the same way a human surface, the eyes and skin and hair and clothes and shoes, look shiny, in certain lights, and this light was that certain light.

I was a joke, an anachronism, the last of my kind, reliant on a breathing system that wasn't even functioning properly any more. I gulped down air in an attempt to re-regularise my breathing, but it was proving hopeless. My lungs were wobbling the same way my eyes were wobbling in their nystagmusic state. They couldn't fit or hold oxygen. And the vitreous humour gel of my eyes had turned to jelly and was wobbling like a jelly. My association of these words in my head, 'gel' and 'jelly', was making this happen, and the metaphoric qualities of this image were translating themselves to my lungs to cause the oxygen-expelling wobble inefficiency in my breathing, incapacitating my ability to take a breath.

The shell simulacra had none of these problems. They weren't breathing, anyway. They just made the exact same actions as a breathing person.

My reliance on oxygen and their lack of reliance on oxygen led me to the most obvious conclusion about my difficulties breathing. Something was in the air. Something in the air was poisoning me. The shell machines – I refused to think of them as people, Jennifer and the others – were poisoning me because I had not transitioned or been replaced. I thought perhaps it was their shiny surface that was exuding some lead-based or other noxious metal-based paint with which the shells were painted.

Why were they doing this? Why did they want me dead, just because I was the last of the old type, the old style of human presentation? I was human, they were shell versions of humans, but we had a common humanity in that we both presented as humans. Couldn't they find common cause with me and stop this poisoning of the air that was killing me? It all seemed so pointless.

But no. Now the wobble-metaphor thought had seeped into my heart, causing my heart to wobble in response. Things were becoming impossible. I might drop to the floor. My legs were going from under me, but still I stood upright.

Perhaps I was beginning to transition.

Perhaps my legs were actually hollow plastic metal-based painted shell legs already and this was what was holding me up.

Mibby I didn't have much longer until I was fully the new type of human, the shell simulacra that everyone else was. Or at least, all the people around me right now. Something horrible was happening, I just couldn't tell what or where it was. Outside, mibby. Millions of people turning into or being replaced by shells of themselves.

That's when Jennifer said to me, Are you OK? You have a look... I mean, your eyes are, like, kind of wobbling.

This pulled me back some distance from the shell thoughts I had been having, and I knew that Jennifer was the internal organs, skin and bone version of herself. But then she was the shell again when I tried to look directly at her. I tried to hold on to the feeling she was herself, her human self, not the shell machine that I kept feeling her to be. It made no sense – it didn't relate to anything I knew about the world, that she might not be herself. I focused to keep this in mind.

I gulped air.

Finally, after an amount of time I could not then and cannot now judge, I was able to cut through everything that was going on and say, quite calmly, as the only other option was to say nothing at all, I think I'm having a panic attack.

You feel you're having a panic attack? Jennifer said.

No, I said, keeping as much calm in my voice as possible, I feel as if I am in the process of dying. That's what I feel. But I think I'm having a panic attack, from what I know about them. They feel like you're dying.

Dying? Dying of what? Jennifer said.

Something horrible... poison... in the air... affecting my heart... a heart attack. My ability to talk calmly and breathe were deserting me.

What can I do?

Nothing. It's happening. It has happened. Triggered. Adrenaline. Coursing through. I looked down at the veins and arteries in my arms, my hands. Oh God, I said. I was in a frozen moment where nothing would move even if I tried to move it. The hideous frozen moment, the worst possible moment to grind to a halt in, this moment, this awful moment, the moment of...

I'll talk, Jennifer said.

No! I said. I mean, yes, yes. Talk. Say something.

I think... Jennifer said, I think you're having a panic attack, too. Can you hear me?

I nodded.

OK. You're having a panic attack. It'll pass, won't it? All things pass, don't they? And you won't be dead. You'll still be alive. After. She nodded. After the panic attack is over. This moment will end. You're feeling, um, flight or fight.

Yes, I said. I feel that. There was a thunderclap. I wasn't sure if it was real or only something I was hearing. I said, It's the end of the fucking world.

I looked up and into Jennifer's eyes. There was still a vestige of the shell in her eyes. I closed my eyes and wished the shell away, wished the shell thought away.

In the dark there was the slightest of slivers of feeling of relief that, perhaps, if I am having a panic attack, and if I had heard other people had had panic attacks, and at some point these people were no longer having a panic attack, at some future moment, at some time *after*, then this could also be true for me, at some point, in the future – not now, not in a now that seemed to be lasting, stretching out, to an unforeseeable point of nowness that led on from this hideous now, the thought that there could be a *then*, in the future, that is not this now, this horror-show now, this chasm of nowness.

Now beat down on me in the form of the lights above us, the glare, the heavy air; the weight of gravity on my head was palpable, perceivable, killing me, concreting my heart, crushing my lungs.

Then it stopped.

I wasn't in *now* any more.

I was in the next moment.

It had finally come, the next moment, the moment *after*.

72

There was a before, then a terrifying now, and now there was an after.

And I hadn't died. I felt euphoric, insanely happy, I laughed and Jennifer looked utterly perplexed.

I was left with the idea that my mind had constructed the shell thought, and the associated cul de sacs of thought that my mind had led me down: the wobble, the lamp, the poison. My mind had done that, as though I had, against my will and better judgement, created these thoughts, told myself these things, written, as it were, these scenarios, these scenes. I was almost more scared of this thought than I had been of the experience itself – that not only had I felt and thought these things, it was I that had planned, composed, edited and proofread this insane story and told it to myself.

I had had a passing strange thought, that the people around me were shell replicas of themselves. My mind had run with this thought, creating sentences which embellished and elaborated the shell thought, and my panic had made those sentences my reality. It was frightening. I suddenly felt frozen in the moment. And in this frozen moment was when a first flash of an idea shot through my mind, that the people in front of me were only characters I had created, perhaps in an Edinburgh Fringe show, and were saying things I simply wanted them to say.

There's an unbearably light moment in *The Unbearable Lightness of Being* – two moments, really – as Kundera feels the need to underline the point, when the protagonist Tomáš and Tomáš's wife Tereza and Tomáš's friend and mistress Sabina and Sabina's lover Franz and Tomáš's son Šimon and Tomáš and Tereza's dog Karenin are outed as characters in a novel – this novel, in fact, *The Unbearable Lightness of Being* – and by extension even Mefisto the pig is not spared in this truth-telling, I suppose. And, so, also, again by extension, this novel, *The Unbearable Lightness of Being*, is just writing, just a novel, just a *story*, as though we, as readers of this novel by Milan Kundera, might not have guessed this. Kundera is inculcating us, the readers, because Kundera knows what's going on, and now we know too, it's just Tomáš and Tereza and Sabina and Franz and Šimon who don't know they are characters in this novel. I suppose, also, that we're supposed to suppose that Karenin and Mefisto understand in whatever way a dog and a pig can that they exist in reality. The human characters in the novel of course understand that Alexei Karenin and Anna Karenina are characters in a novel, Tolstoy's novel, in a way that Karenin and Anna cannot possibly guess, but, then, where does that get us? Also, this Edinburgh Fringe show idea.

Well.

Curious little thought.

It flared and then faded.

Actually, most of this that I've just told you is lies, too. Well, lies of omission. What I mean is, if you really want to know, I spent most of 1999, from the June onwards, burning CDs of music stolen from musicians via Napster. Whole days got taken up with that.

7

15 hours to go

From a.a.strang@molextrics.co.uk
Fri 31 Dec 1999 at 15:15

Sun up on the millennium. Dude, I can see it.

From craigstewart@hotmail.com
Sat 1 Jan 2000 at 05:12

The big plans are for the sunrise. Sunrise on
Kiribati on the millennium is a big big deal
here for the people making the arrangements. The
Kiribatians and the press people. It's not like
they can do a big firework display, but I guess
there isn't a biogger fireworks display ever than
the SUN coming up, MAN, so I see their point.
I'm guessing this is going to look a lot more
impressive than a bunch of press and tv journos
getting smashed on a beach at midnight with just
a few twigs on fire for heat and light.

From a.a.strang@molextrics.co.uk
Fri 31 Dec 1999 at 15:12

Swimming to Cambodia.

From craigstewart@hotmail.com
Sat 1 Jan 2000 at 05:08

Yeah, that was the GFT, wasn't it? Seems a long
time ago now.

From a.a.strang@molextrics.co.uk
Fri 31 Dec 1999 at 15:07

Give in. Come in to the water, Spalding, man.

From craigstewart@hotmail.com
Sat 1 Jan 2000 at 05:06

Oh, God, no, I was so drunk that time. no I
don't think I been that drunk since, dude. But
the booze and the maidens of the South Seas are
calling to me siren songs.

From a.a.strang@molextrics.co.uk
Fri 31 Dec 1999 at 15:03

Your writing is going a wee bit astray, mate.
Are you getting smashed? Is this the return
of... SMASHEDMAN?!?!?!

From craigstewart@hotmail.com
Sat 1 Jan 2000 at 05: 01

Hey, Nostro-damus, the end of the world did NOT
occur on the 4th of July 1999. Idda noticed it
if it had. I had a wild day that day, definitely
Unapocalypsey. She was beautiful, man.

From a.a.strang@molextrics.co.uk
Fri 31 Dec 1999 at 14:58

I think we may have been through that already,
dude. Say this living death of the end of history
where nothing ever happens of any consequence is
IT, man. We're in the end days when nothing everywhere doesn't happen from now on.

From craigstewart@hotmail.com
Sat 1 Jan 2000 at 04:55

Are we all going to die on Millennium night. Just
thought I'd throw that in.

From a.a.strang@molextrics.co.uk
Fri 31 Dec 1999 at 14:54

Last night I started laughing because a few days
before I was looking through some old Friends tape
and Chandler, just before writing up what was wrong
with Rachael, the one where he's 'written' a short
story, describes his laptop: 'check it out... 12.8
kbs modem, 120 Megabytes of RAM...' anyway, all very
funny because so out of date, Friends lives up to
becoming hip retro reference... Come on. Big Leb-
owski. Best film of the last ten years...written and
directed by people called Coen. Aw mom, it's Tommy's
turn to overthrow a Third World country. I did it
last week. I got drunk a few nights ago on own and
then Decided to see how weird a web site I could
visit. Not very weird. Did you ever work out the
third word with gry as an ending? Over xmas I watched
It's a wonderful life and cried my little heart out.

I watched Elephant Man the other day and man was I
bubbling. Is bubbling a word you use for crying?
It's Scots maybe and can be rendered burbbln.

From craigstewart@hotmail.com
Sat 1 Jan 2000 at 04:50

Anyway, I watched Saving Private Ryan the other
night on this movie channel and I liked it so
much more than I did before it was like I had seen
a different film. That is a weird experience.

From craigstewart@hotmail.com
Sat 1 Jan 2000 at 04.45

student: 'Rock and roll will never die.'
teacher: 'Actually Bob, recent studies show that
rock and roll is in fact dying.'
student: 'Uh, what?'

Come on baby put out my fire. I like that one.
I'm burning up here. Put out my fire. She could
put out my fire if you know what I mean.

Which words end in gry? Apparently there are
three, not just two.

From a.a.strang@molextrics.co.uk
Fri 31 Dec 1999 at 14:41

Remember, don't fear the reaper. Actually,
due to a typing error in Blue Oyster Cult's
secretarial pool, it was really 'do fear the

reaper', if only all those Satanist death metal guys realised THAT. Then where would we be?

I tried to get on a theme for a second, but came up blank except for these other lyric mistypes:

It's NOT only rock and roll

Come on baby, PUT OUT my fire

UNLIKE a rolling stone

This is going nowhere, I feel; my favourite place.

No curry Friday night? No curry? Mmm. Curry pie. Mmmm. American pie.

Mmm. Mathematical pie...

Pies, really. Come on, work with me, people.

From craigstewart@hotmail.com
Sat 1 Jan 2000 at 04:35

Yeah I don't get many e-mails lately either. Probably because I don't e-mail people. I lazy.

From a.a.strang@molextrics.co.uk
Fri 31 Dec 1999 at 14:30

Know of Damien Hirst?? Man, I got kicked out of his bar in London one time, for not being cool enough. Getting kicked out of Pharmacy was one of the least interesting things that ever happened to me in London, and man there is some competition for that non-event.

From craigstewart@hotmail.com
Sat 1 Jan 2000 at 04:25

Ever heard of Damien Hirst, the crazy artist? His recent controversial exhibition in New York is making waves. One of the condemned artists (Holy Mary painting avec elephant dung) is a Nigerian (?) guy from Manchester. There's something almost every day in the NY Times about how people are angry.

You should find out about David Foster Wallace. He is massive here. Ethan Hawke (star of Dead Poets Society and Before Sunrise and father to Uma's child) is a novelist. I wonder how he got published. My mom read his book (The Hottest State) and said it's not all that bad. Before Sunrise has all these brilliantly constructed scenes. It's very carefully done without being cheesy I think. Pinball scene blows me away. And I like Julie Delpy. She speaks French. That's cool. Last night at the bar I wrote the four words Hound of the Baskervilles on a piece of paper. Help me. The madness must end.

From a.a.strang@molextrics.co.uk
Fri 31 Dec 1999 at 14:05

Did I tell you The Onion got a namecheck in the Sunday Times this week? They called it a 'slacker magazine', where running out of ice cream is considered of equal importance to your relationship ending or your parents dying.

Mmmm. Ice cream.

From craigstewart@hotmail.com
Sat 1 Jan 2000 at 04:00

Really looks like I will go to Arizona for a while. Japan is just an option. I don't really see myself living there--it's just a cool thing to say to people.

From a.a.strang@molextrics.co.uk
Fri 31 Dec 1999 at 13:56

Don't go to Japan, man. There's something about that that tells me it would be a bad move. Something like, five years from now in Kyoto: 'Yeah a few years back I wrote a book, but I never did anything more about it. I came to Japan.' The only good thing about Japan is Tokyo and Kyoto are anagrams, man. That's not a good enough reason to actually go there.

From craigstewart@hotmail.com
Sat 1 Jan 2000 at 03:52

Clean slate to e-mail. Have been having problems with my internet connection. Can't seem to get hotmail to work on my laptop. I ask for your address and you send me nothing. I really do

have an article for you to see that you'll like
and if I say that I'll scan the thing and send
it through cyberspace for you then, well, we're
kidding ourselves.

From a.a.strang@molextrics.co.uk
Fri 31 Dec 1999 at 13:48

Carrey was in the audience heavily disguised as
some sort of hippy survivor and when his name was
called (for Truman) this hippy guy (which the
cameras had kept picking out and you thought, as
he wanted us to... well, it's MTV) strolls up to
the podium... and it is Jim. He says in a drawl
how his success has made him able to be himself,
kept toking on a cigarillo, big belly beneath a
tie-dye string vest, Peace an Love signs to the
audience, then Mike Myers had to help him off
stage. Wait a goddamn minute... was this satire?

From craigstewart@hotmail.com
Sat 1 Jan 2000 at 03:45

Did I tell you I went to see The Thin Red Line
for the fifth time the other night? I'm thinking
about starting a society club gang clique group
circle klan band type thing. It's between The
Thin Red Line and Dirty Dancing. I haven't
Decided yet. Saw Koyaanisqatsi as well. Did
I tell you that? My recent memory sucks but I
can recall what I had for lunch in first grade.

From a.a.strang@molextrics.co.uk
Fri 31 Dec 1999 at 13:34

The other night on Sex And The City amazing developments!! One of the women (the brunette who works in the gallery) visited a great artist she really admired intent on doing anything to secure a showing by him. When she arrives he says he is going to show her his latest and greatest work, which is revealed to be a set of split beaver shots entitled Cunt (1, 2, 3, etc...) Then his aging wife arrives and says something like 'How do you like Cunt?' and then the artist asks the gallery gal to pose for him. Cue the aging wife: 'I bet you have a lovely cunt.' I always thought that it was a banned word on Brit TV. I looked on in disbelief. The joke ended with the SATC team trying to work out which Cunt the gallery gal was at the opening. Unbelievable.

Why is it the bit that keeps coming back to me from Tootsie is this totally meaningless doesnt advance plot or character vignette where Terri is at a party but gets locked in the bathroom for an hour by mistake? She finally makes it out, totally stressed. 'Didn't ANYONE hear me SCREAMING?' says Terri.

From craigstewart@hotmail.com
Sat 1 Jan 2000 at 03:29

stop playing charades you sad bastard

From a.a.strang@molextrics.co.uk
Fri 31 Dec 1999 at 13:28

did you go bananas last new years eve? i had a
very quiet one playing charades with a couple
of friends, wasnt even, like, strip charades on
cocaine or nothin... did i ever tell you about
the time i dreamed about the old group taking
place but we were all sitting barefoot like
suzannah? the thing was it felt really scary and
ominous this barefoot thing like it was a cult
thing and we were being forced to be barefoot

From craigstewart@hotmail.com
Sat 1 Jan 2000 at 03:25

Your guy Dougay McLean wrote Caledonia on a
beach in Portufgal, didn't he.

so anyway i had this weird dream last night
that found a few of us from class at a pub and
hannah (is her name a palindrome or did i spell
it wrong) wanted to go out for japanese (is
that spelled correctly i'm a crummy speller i
suspect) food and then to a dire straits concert
but you didn't want to go and so we didn't go
but i did want to go and i missed having tempura
or something and listening to dire straits live
because of you thanks a lot mr selfish

From a.a.strang@molextrics.co.uk
Fri 31 Dec 1999 at 13:24

Keep your beer, man. We can take it YOU say
exile from the self is the realest exile.

From a.a.strang@molextrics.co.uk
Fri 31 Dec 1999 at 13:23

So the poem is about exile from the self?

From craigstewart@hotmail.com
Sat 1 Jan 2000 at 03:23

Is now.

From a.a.strang@molextrics.co.uk
Fri 31 Dec 1999 at 13:23

Realest is a word?

From craigstewart@hotmail.com
Sat 1 Jan 2000 at 03:23

Doesn't someone say something about the exile
from the self being the only real exile. Sorry,
though, can't remember who now and if I check
the Internet as opposed to type to you, I may
drop my beer.

From a.a.strang@molextrics.co.uk
Fri 31 Dec 1999 at 13:22

Yeah, you'd know. I've made it all the way from
Ayr to Glasgow to Edinburgh in my measly life.
You're the traveller. Yet my internal exile is
real enough. Your exile is hyperreal.

From craigstewart@hotmail.com
Sat 1 Jan 2000 at 03:21

Yeah. Does. Kinda.

From a.a.strang@molextrics.co.uk
Fri 31 Dec 1999 at 13:20

Yeah, 5 continents man. I donno. The world out
there, I get the impression it smells like dung.

From craigstewart@hotmail.com
Sat 1 Jan 2000 at 03:13

Exile I know all about. Oh man, some television
journalist guy just showed up and he thinks it's
a cool thing to be wearing two different color of
socks. Dude, I gotta tell you, that is not cool.
Look around you. NO ONE else has any socks on at
all, this is the pacific south seas, man. The dude
is an idiot, clearly.

From a.a.strang@molextrics.co.uk
Fri 31 Dec 1999 at 13:10

I went back to the RLS poem there for a second.
Edinburgh gets to be the city of the dead. The
illustrious dead? He says kings and other notables
earlier, right. Am I getting this?; Or is it a
city dead to him now he is in the South Seas?
Certainly a song of the exile. Hankering for his
homeland? Mmm. Mibby.

From craigstewart@hotmail.com
Sat 1 Jan 2000 at 03:09

No, we can't. Pool or writing. Jesus. Christ,
dude.

From a.a.strang@molextrics.co.uk
Fri 31 Dec 1999 at 13:09

Dude. No we cannot. That was always one of your
favourites. Man, you CAN NOT! We can't play
pool, and we can't write.

From craigstewart@hotmail.com
Sat 1 Jan 2000 at 03:07

Oh, man, we CANNOT play pool.

From a.a.strang@molextrics.co.uk
Fri 31 Dec 1999 at 13:05

Yeah, I seem to remember we also talked about
our abiloity to play pool.

From craigstewart@hotmail.com
Sat 1 Jan 2000 at 03:02

Yes! The Fonz. You had said something about
staying cool in Aus and then we had been like
Aaaaaayyyyyyy. Aaaaaaayyyyyy. Giving it loads on
the Fonzie front. And then I said, but of course
The Fonz is not cool. You were like, Fonzie's
NOT cool? Then your eyes starting serching the
space in front of you, left to right and back
again as you searched your mind and you were
so obviously going, Spends a lot of time in
a Male toilet, hangs out with nerdles, has no
ambition... HEY, HOLD ON A FUCKIN MINUTE: FONZIE
IS NOT COOL! Man, the revealation in your eyes.

From a.a.strang@molextrics.co.uk
Fri 31 Dec 1999 at 12:57

Eh... something about Arthur Fonzarella, if I'm
not mistaken.

Enough with the sausages. Do you know what I was
thinking about recently? That last conversation
we had before you headed to Aus, dude. You were
leaving the pub and you were Nixon getting on
the presidential copter with the waved peace
signs. Funny. But the conversation we had had,
do you remember?

From craigstewart@hotmail.com
Sat 1 Jan 2000 at 02:54

Not a sausage. What does it matter, man? The
Soviet Union COLLAPSED, man. Russia, what's
that? Is that enough with the sausages for now?

From a.a.strang@molextrics.co.uk
Fri 31 Dec 1999 at 12:52

Is that right? Anyway, this Yeltsin/Putin thing.
Are we getting any reactions?

From craigstewart@hotmail.com
Sat 1 Jan 2000 at 02:50

Very literary and posh. You've become a right
old posh sausage in yer auld age.

From a.a.strang@molextrics.co.uk
Fri 31 Dec 1999 at 12:49

Not a smoked sausage. Probably the usual stuff.
Milne's or the Café Royal.

From craigstewart@hotmail.com
Sat 1 Jan 2000 at 02:48

What are your plans for Hogmanay anyway? Talking
of hogs.

From a.a.strang@molextrics.co.uk
Fri 31 Dec 1999 at 12:47

Not a smoked sausage.

From craigstewart@hotmail.com
Sat 1 Jan 2000 at 02:46

So, got anything for me.

From craigstewart@hotmail.com
Sat 1 Jan 2000 at 02:46

Ah, right! OK, I can see the Robert Louie Louie
Stevenson connection would be the angle to go for.

From a.a.strang@molextrics.co.uk
Fri 31 Dec 1999 at 12:40

It was written by RLS, thinking of Edinburgh
while he was on this island when it was called
the Gilberts.

From craigstewart@hotmail.com
Sat 1 Jan 2000 at 02:37

I guess because of the controversy that Kiribati
kicked up a few years ago by jumping the date line
so they could be firast to the millennium instead
of back of the queue. People went CARAAYZEEE
over hear about that, like the Micronesia Third
World War was gonna break out. A lot of Japanese
soldiers would be coming out of the island jungle
woodwork saying ha toild you so, WAR NEVER ENDS,
MAN. Also, I'm being syndicated or something
like that back to the Scotsman and they wanted a
Scottish person (well, via WI ansd WA) to make
some sort of connection between Kiribati (which
has kicked up some controversy over this side
of the world taking their independent decision
to jump the international date line to be first
and not last. The Pacific Islands is our back
yard, you know? My ed usedta be Scotsman and he
made some deal to be first with the news for the
paper. Sends me out here with this

The tropics vanish, and meseems that I,
From Halkerside, from topmost Allermuir,
Or steep Caerketton, dreaming gaze again.
Far set in fields and woods, the town I see
Spring gallant from the shallows of her smoke,
Cragged, spired, and turreted, her virgin fort
Beflagged. About, on seaward-drooping hills,
New folds of city glitter. Last, the Forth
Wheels ample waters set with sacred isles,
And populous Fife smokes with a score of towns.

There, on the sunny frontage of a hill,
Hard by the house of kings, repose the dead,
My dead, the ready and the strong of word.
Their works, the salt-encrusted, still survive;
The sea bombards their founded towers; the night
Thrills pierced with their strong lamps. The artificers,
One after one, here in this grated cell,
Where the rain erases, and the rust consumes,
Fell upon lasting silence. Continents
And continental oceans intervene;
A sea uncharted, on a lampless isle,
Environs and confines their wandering child
In vain. The voice of generations dead
Summons me, sitting distant, to arise,
My numerous footsteps nimbly to retrace,
And, all mutation over, stretch me down
In that denoted city of the dead.

And told me to make the story from this angle.
What do you make of it?

OK, I can see the poem has some sort of connection,
but I don't know it. What's the deal?

From a.a.strang@molextrics.co.uk
Fri 31 Dec 1999 at 12:35

Hey, man, I had my reasons, I don't need excuses.
Excuses are for the little people, and I'm a big
person. BIG ME. Hey, man, EFF U.

Why did a Perth paper want to send you out to
Kiribati anyway?

From craigstewart@hotmail.com
Sat 1 Jan 2000 at 02:33

Have you been drifting around the Internet for
two years and that's the excuse you can come up
with. Duuuude.

From a.a.strang@molextrics.co.uk
Fri 31 Dec 1999 at 12:09

Dude, I did provide a service. Like paying for
reassurance. It was an insurance policy. Getting
me in made them feel safer, which made them
actually safer.

From craigstewart@hotmail.com
Sat 1 Jan 2000 at 01:58

You are just so... FRAUDULENT! I LOVE IT.
Duuuuuuuude.

From a.a.strang@molextrics.co.uk
Fri 31 Dec 1999 at 11:43

Sorry, man, not at liberty to say. I'm thinking
the computers have not failed and you replying
is proof and that's all I need, instead of you
re[lying directly to what I'm asking.

From craigstewart@hotmail.com
Sat 1 Jan 2000 at 01:23

Man, how much are these idiots paying you for
this shit?

From a.a.strang@molextrics.co.uk
Fri 31 Dec 1999 at 11:01

THE Y2K BUG DIDN"T EXIST. THERE WAS NO Y2K BUG!
IS NO Y2K BUG. THERE SIMPLY IS NO Y2K BUG. That's
the whole point, dude. And you could confirm this
for me by giving me a simple answer to a simple
question. Are the computers around you failing?
And I mean in a more general way than somehow
making you incapable to hearing me WHEN I AM
BASICALLY SHOUTRING AT YOU TO GIVE ME A DAMN
ANSWRR, DUDE, ARE COMPUTERS FAILING??????????

From craigstewart@hotmail.com
Sat 1 Jan 2000 at 00:45

So, let me get this straight. You have done
ABSOLUTELY NOTHIN in terms of sorting out the
Y2K bug???!!! Dude!

From a.a.strang@molextrics.co.uk
Fri 31 Dec 1999 at 10:40

Patrick?? He was the one that told me that
there was absolutely nothing to be done. Forgive me that I have not a Scooby what I am
supposed to know about it, but he says, basically, info for children level, he says computers would have had to have been in existence (in a way we recognise) in 1900 for the
problem of the clock ticking over from 1999
to 2000 existing as a bug. Even worse if computers had been existing in 1800, 1700, 1600.
But then, if they had been, well, doesn't that

mean the first bug would have been noted and sorted out as 1699 became 1700 and all the 99s to 00s in their turn. ALSO. ANSWER ME! HAVE THE COMPUTERS FAILED? I have a weird feeling you are not answering me because they have failed in a very specific way that does not allow my messages asking or your messages answering getting through. I know you are still communicating with the outside world, because you are e-mailing me right now, but it just seems weird that you are not answering my most obvious and pressing question!!

From craigstewart@hotmail.com
Sat 1 Jan 2000 at 00:38

But didn't Patrick have you doing SOMETHING? Just for appearances' sake?

From a.a.strang@molextrics.co.uk
Fri 31 Dec 1999 at 10:27

I haven't stopped, except now, talking to you. Actually, you know what the truth is. I've told you, there's nothing to it. I have been basically doing nothing for two years. Thinking up a few hoaxes and schemes, some other moneymaking ideas. Mostly I just sit on the Internet drifting around, scrolling down. One day, this will be everyones' lives. Scrolling, scrolling, scrolling. One rabbit hole after another.

From craigstewart@hotmail.com
Sat 1 Jan 2000 at 00:14

You work for Mole. Isn't that electrician? So,
you feeling confident that the whole Y2K thing
has been done up like a kipper for your bosses?
I suppose it's been pretty flat out?

From a.a.strang@molextrics.co.uk
Fri 31 Dec 1999 at 10:10

I told you, I'm a visionary not a plumber.

From craigstewart@hotmail.com
Sat 1 Jan 2000 at 00.07

Don't take my word, but I think you're using beta
the wrong way there, futurology genius!

From a.a.strang@molextrics.co.uk
Fri 31 Dec 1999 at 10:06

Nah, dude, you're not getting what these guys are
into. They're not short sighted but they just
want to know what the next step is. Five steps on
is no use to them cuz they know they have to beta
all the steps in between.

From craigstewart@hotmail.com
Sat 1 Jan 2000 at 00:05

Not fifty years time, man?

From a.a.strang@molextrics.co.uk
Fri 31 Dec 1999 at 10:05

Yeah, you're funny, dude. I told you, Patrick has
been advising me. Mole says I have the insight
that means more than technical crapola. He sees
me as some kind of futurology genius, I think, I
think they may be keeping me on after the balloon
goes up as some sort of consultant adviser or
something telling what the world going to be
like in twenty years time. Still can't work out
how a numpty like you got the gig. Also, did you
see my question about Y2K? I asked you if the
computers and computer systems around you were
failing or not, if that happened or might happen
after midnight? HAVE THE COMPUTERS FAILED?

From a.a.strang@molextrics.co.uk
Fri 31 Dec 1999 at 10:00

Coming up 10 am on the 31st . I'm not in work,
so up quite early for me. Got a lot to do today!
I don't have to go into Mole until later and
then he thinks all the work has been done, which
it has in the sense that there's nothing else
to achieve. If it goes tits up at our midnight,
there's nothing much we can do about it now. I've
told them that I've made all the preparation and
adjustments I can. Don't know if they believe
me. I have to go in if they see anyting going
wrongin the few hours we have left. Me, I'm just
crossing all fingers and toes now as it stands,.

From craigstewart@hotmail.com
Fri 31 Dec 1999 at 23:59.

Pretty much got it, dude, yip. It is beautiful, you knew and I knew it was going to be. Nothing's blue just at the minute. We're just coming up to midnight and where we are out on the beach is pretty dark. I thought there would be more cameras and stuff and big lights lighting everything up, but where I've been told to come to, it's mostly print journos and a few loicals and just the lights from a few screens, like me tippy tapping away writing to you. The big celebration seems to be being kept for dawn of the furst day of the new millennium. Of course, with my renowned ability to be on every winning side (NOT!) I was hanging with all these people from Millennium-Live. You heard about that, the alt prog from 2000Today, set up by the American Live Aid guy. Fell apart three days ago. Now all the camera guys and presenters and other people are spending their time getting WASTED. Millenium Dead: Human-ity's (last?) Broadcast. The bunch of them are just along the beach utterly wasted already, and I admit I've been with them most of the day. Hey, it's just struck me that there is some mad cele-bration at midnight and 2000Today are whopping it up grand style. But I think they are also wait-ing for the sort of ritual I've seen rehearsing for dawn. More visual, I guess, as they haven't exactly arranged Sydney harbour bridge-style fire-worlks out here in the slap bang middle of fucking NOWHERE. Nah, probably not as we are on this kind of headland (I think) that will be where the dawn

will first fall across the land. I better send some
e-mails back to my ed, by the way, on the devastation wrought by the MillenniumDead fiasco, be back
at cha in a mo. What time's it where you are?

From a.a.strang@molextrics.co.uk
Fri 31 Dec 1999 at 09:54

Yeah, I know what you mean. What's it like over
there. I just can't imagine it, somehow. I mean,
I know youll be breathing the same air and walking
on ground (sand, right?) and it'll be kinda like
Uist, I suspect. Remember that time we were on
Berneray and the water and white sand and it did
look like a Caribbean island or somewhere in the
south seas. The water so blue and clear, or clear
then blue as it got deeper. It's like that, right?
Hey, my boss has a Caribbean Island, and I mean
owns one. Also, dude, have any of the computers
failed? anyone's? or look like they might?

From craigstewart@hotmail.com
Fri 31 Dec 1999 at 23:50

I don't see Kiribati in terms of your linear
Western time man. I see five individual balls of
light functioning as one. I see essence. You
are so narrow. Yeah, I am living it up here, but
only because there's nothing else to fucking do.
No good cinema. No bookstores. No TV in English. Mass media is my life. I am a child of pop
culture. I am a Gen Xer. I would rather be in
England... Scotland, even, if I had to...

From a.a.strang@molextrics.co.uk
Fri 31 Dec 1999 at 09:48

You bring up an interesting point about functional literacy. When can you actually 'speak' a language? When you can order pizza and buy milk and pay a gas bill in that language? When you can make a joke in the language? (This is quite a good test.) When you can formulate an economic policy for dealing with teenage unemployment for the country's government? (It was Tommy's turn to do that this week.) When you can write a major three part documentary about the place of bassoons in that country's culture, or an hilarious haiku satirising the mayor of the capital city? Interesting. I read that there are now 750 million speakers of the English as a second language in the world and this for the first time surpasses number of the speakers with the English as first language, so we all talk like this now, not the conjugating verbs et cetera get used to it the buddy.

P.S. What is your actual time frame in Kiri? Like, a year? You're living it up, right?

From craigstewart@hotmail.com
Fri 31 Dec 1999 at 23:44

Some German people are here and when my producer introduced me to some German diplomat guy and told him I spoke German which is only partly true and I said the only things I could remember and then the German diplomat guy shook my hand and pretty much crushed every bone in it and I think that was his way of telling me: 'YOU're German SUCKs.'

From a.a.strang@molextrics.co.uk
Fri 31 Dec 1999 at 09:43

I have been laughing at the thought of you laughing and now I'm laughing at how weak this is and we are a coupla grinning sniggering laughing jokin horsin around guys and satellites and a telecommunication miracle of the global village was invented for this??

From craigstewart@hotmail.com
Fri 31 Dec 1999 at 23:42

You should be on the TV this e-mail is so fucking funny.

From a.a.strang@molextrics.co.uk
Fri 31 Dec 1999 at 09:40

Me too! I cannot fuckin believe it I spent about 2 hours answering and making points in response to one of your other e-mails and then the fucking network went down and I lost it all man and man was there some stuff in there. I will now attempt to go over the main point but fuck man i mean fuck i don't know. FUCK. THIS SUCKS. I can't do it.

From craigstewart@hotmail.com
Fri 31 Dec 1999 at 23:37

Piece of shit computer erased my message to you and that pisses me off man.

From a.a.strang@molextrics.co.uk
Fri 31 Dec 1999 at 09:34

Man, there really is a movie called Striptease
Baby Dolls from Cleveland Meet the Unkillables.
I wonder how they got on? That program Movies
Movies Movies, it could have been a big hit. If
only they had emphasised it was about movies.
On the bright side, Beavis and Butt-Head did
America on tv this weekend and man was there
a very funny joke about not ending a sentence
with a preposition. Man was it funny. I'm
concentrating on how funny this was.

From craigstewart@hotmail.com
Fri 31 Dec 1999 at 23:23

Being here is so isolated. It's another planet.
I miss English speaking communities and food
that doesn't live in a shell.

From a.a.strang@molextrics.co.uk
Fri 31 Dec 1999 at 09:22

It's spelled Luton but boy did your spelling
make me laugh. Why? It's not funny and you make
a wholly adequate attempt at it. A couple of
days ago on the street I really pissed off a
woman who was doing a 'survey' but really trying
to sell me a holiday. Her first question: Do you
like holidays? Yes or No. I said no. Man did
that fuck up the rest of the form/questionnaire/
scam. Everyone loves holidays, man. Who the fuck
ARE you? Man, she was not happy with me. She

persevered. What was my favourite type of holiday?
I don't like holidays, remember?

Her(angry): Oh. Well what kinda holidays do you take?
Me: I took a beach holiday once.
Her: RIGHT! (Now we're getting somewhere look on
face, goes to tick beach holidays box).
Me: Yeah, I didn't like it.
Her: (Silent fury.)

From craigstewart@hotmail.com
Fri 31 Dec 1999 at 23:15

Went to British pub as well just before I left for
here, it was filled with British people and I ate
Scotch eggs which one of my friends ordered and
I talked to this guy bartender and his girlfriend
waitress and they were both from London (Lewton?)
and they couldn't have cared less that I lived in
England and man did they not care and they were
just not interested.

From a.a.strang@molextrics.co.uk
Fri 31 Dec 1999 at 09:06

THERE'S A SONG BY THE CHEMICAL BROTHERS AND NOEL
GALLAGHER CALLED 'HOW DOES IT FEEL LIKE?' AND I
WAS THINKING THIS IS THE BEST GRAMMATICAL ERROR
IN ROCK SINCE 'I CAN'T GET NO SATISFACTION'. HUH?
I hate using upper case. Why did I do that? We get
older. That's the adventure, apparently. I feel
weird today, like it's the end of the world and
I don't care. I watched Fahrenheit 451 a coupla

weeks ago. It is a disconcerting movie. I was in the library last week reading about Last Year in Mareinbad and what Resnais said about that (characters exist only within the timeframe of the movie, and temporal reality is not suspended as some believe, but is constructed as an instantaneous moment or something).

From craigstewart@hotmail.com
Fri 31 Dec 1999 at 23:04

Went to see Fahrenheit 451 the other day.

From a.a.strang@molextrics.co.uk
Fri 31 Dec 1999 at 09:03

Apparently, due to inflation and a cost of living increase headaches are now only available for $17.50. Minimum. So that song no longer, uh, you know, rings true. I heard there's a film coming out called The Replacements. Not a rock biopic of the band though, I don't think.

From craigstewart@hotmail.com
Fri 31 Dec 1999 at 22:58

Did I mention? Finished watching this season of Sopranos and now I'm experiencing withdrawal. What a headache man. Great old Replacements song: I Bought A Headache. Lyrics are: I bought a headache (punk guitar), headache (punk guitar), headache (guitar again), for $8.50 I bought a headache (more guitar).

103

From a.a.strang@molextrics.co.uk
Fri 31 Dec 1999 at 08:58

Hurrah, you are back, my computer has been
lovebugged. I have not been getting my e-mails. It
is a fucking disaster! Is this thing on? I think
it is now. Hello hello hello. Test. One two. One
two. One two. Three.

From craigstewart@hotmail.com
Fri 31 Dec 1999 at 22:58

I have been sending e-mails. I do not think you are
getting my e-mails. I do not know what is wrong with
the e-mail. I am getting pissed off at the e-mail.

From craigstewart@hotmail.com
Fri 31 Dec 1999 at 22:58

Are you getting these? I just sent you two e-mails
that and I'm not going to type out another long
e-mail just to have it not make it to you either.
What the hell is wrong with what seemed to be a
pretty reliable e-mail system? Because this e-mail
contains no valuable information I will not be surprised if it makes it to you without delay.

From craigstewart@hotmail.com
Fri 31 Dec 1999 at 22:58

I thought I sent you an e-mail yesterday. What the
hell happened to that e-mail? Went out with friend
last night before I came here who thinks Jews not
only control everything but will put computer chips

in our wrists and manipulate Americans that way
and that will be the mark of the beast and he's
moving to Mexico because of this and I would have
asked the waitress for more popcorn but that
probably wouldn't have cheered him up and why are
all my friends there so CRAZY?

From a.a.strang@molextrics.co.uk
Fri 31 Dec 1999 at 08:58

Yeah, I meant to tell you: I have decided on a
radical change of approach to my comms. I gotta
tell you, man, you think that's junk, but I know
this is the writing of the future. You just
don't understand... I'm too advanced, man... in
my book, I'd have to say to you:

```
*^^^*><><><><>>:::<><:<:<:{*&*&*&*&*&*}}}
><(*(*(*&*(*&(*^&*^*&^*&(^*&^
><><(*(*^^^^%^%&%&*&^&^&%&$*^*$(
(**&^)*(^_&(*^)^%$*^&%)*&^_(+
```

Man, if you don't KNOW AND FEEL why that is
POETRY, MAN, YOU KNOW nothing. NOTHING, man.
Bored with this now. OK, I'm only kidding. I will
try and send you it in Mac files, and as a last
resort, as the longest e-mail I've ever sent.

From craigstewart@hotmail.com
Fri 31 Dec 1999 at 22:57

When I open your files they are all computer
junk. What gives?

From a.a.strang@molextrics.co.uk
Fri 31 Dec 1999 at 08:58

Hey, there's a website for Magnolia the way
there was for American Beauty! I vaguely remember The BNBs. I didn't think they were that bad
news...

From craigstewart@hotmail.com
Fri 31 Dec 1999 at 22:38

In Magnolia, The kid not answering the quiz
show answers was very Bad News Bears where kid
won't throw ball because he's mad at Daddy. Do
you know The Bad News Bears? They are, inter-
estingly enough, bad news.

From a.a.strang@molextrics.co.uk
Fri 31 Dec 1999 at 08:58

THERE'S THIS BUTTON CALLED ATTACH AND YOU
GO TO THE INTERNET AND PUT THE POINTER ON
A PICTURE AND RIGHT CLICK AND IT SAYS 'SAVE
PICTURE AS' AND I DO AND THEN I GO TO THIS
SAVED FILE IN THE ATTACH WINDOW AND PRESS
OPEN AND HEY PRESTO...

From craigstewart@hotmail.com
Fri 31 Dec 1999 at 22:38

How do you put pictures in your e-mail man?
You're just showing off. The closest I can come
to a picture in an e-mail is this:

```
  **          **
       **
  **          **
     **     **
       **
```

That's supposed to be me smiling. Here is your house:

```
        ************
        **          **
        **          **
        **          **
        **          **
        **          **
        **          **
        **          **
        ************
```

This is fun.

From a.a.strang@molextrics.co.uk
Fri 31 Dec 1999 at 08:57

Do you ever listen to the tape? Sopranos is a big
topic of discussion here at the moment as aguy I
work with finally got a long play video and has
become a Sopranos nutcase from my tapes. We are all
awaiting the next season with bated breath.

From craigstewart@hotmail.com
Fri 31 Dec 1999 at 22:38

It's nice to see that high quality American TV like
The Renegade makes it to Scotland. Man does that

show SUCK. John Stamos, another American hero actor, looks exactly like that guy. A drunk girl told me I looked like John Stamos and that because I was wearing what she called a medallion I must be either a rock star or Canadian. Did I tell you this story already? I think I mentioned John Stamos. I just don't recall man. It's that crazy Canadian rock star lifestyle.

From a.a.strang@molextrics.co.uk
Fri 31 Dec 1999 at 08:55

The computer does it. OK computer. Now I'm freaking out. We're in Frank Zappa territory here. What is your attitude to Frank Zappa? Mine is: it's time to leave the party when it starts to wind down, get dopey and the guy in the corner who hasn't said anything all night goes for his inside pocket and says, quietly, Hey, is anybody here into Frank Zappa?

When I think about it, maybe Frank Zappa was some weird code for some great drugs or a sex thing, and I always walked out at that point. Damn. Sudden thoughts of generational issues, like, an older generation felt uneasy and disconcerted when weird things happened, but younger embraced it??

Man, I was watching tv a few nights ago and you weren't on but this beard reminded me of you. You're gonna hate this: You ARE Lorenzo Lamas AS The Renegade. Do you know that show?

From craigstewart@hotmail.com
Fri 31 Dec 1999 at 08:38

how do you do that where you give an e-mail
address that's actually a link I can click and
then use? That's awesome.

Was thinking about books and movies. Nabokov
thought of Lolita in terms of a cinematic book.
Why? Christopher Isherwood practically invented
the modern externalised novel with 'I am a camera'.
Kundera said that what he liked about 'The Unbearable Lightness of Being' movie is that it left out
everything that is essential to the novel. All
films do this with all books, but the point is that
both forms (formats?) have the same form: raise a
question, delay the answer. Narrative. We're all
suckers for that. Also, people set up websites in
which they write scripts for their favourite soap
operas FOR AMUSEMENT. Did you know about this? Why
do I know about this? I don't want to know about
this! Did you know about this?

From a.a.strang@molextrics.co.uk
Fri 31 Dec 1999 at 08:53

I am trying to imagine what a REAL laugh riot would
be like. Laughs of all sorts being watercannoned
along the street, a nightstick crashing over the
bloodied head of a laugh...

How come all your e-mails arrive timed 8.38. Is
that to do with landlines or something?? ARE YOU

109

THERE?/?????? I love the idiom guy. It's so easy to construct, you dont even have to try to say anything. It writes itself.

Example. Call. 'We have to call a halt to calling a spade a spade. You can't call my bluff that it doesn't call everything into question. We have to call it a day, call it quits, hey, let's call the whole thing off. When it comes to name calling the call of nature, so to speak, does not call the shots, and we have to ask, who calls the tune and when will they be called to account? It's a close call, but that's when we have to say: don't call us, we'll call you.'

From craigstewart@hotmail.com
Fri 31 Dec 1999 at 08:38

Watched The Thin Red Line one time with stoner friend who smoked so much pot I got a contact high and then The Thin Red Line became super funny and pretentious. HA! That's a laugh riot man.

From a.a.strang@molextrics.co.uk
Fri 31 Dec 1999 at 08:50

brewerfan69, Hey, you grew up in the eighties and you like The Smiths too... that's SUCH a coincidence... I scare myself with my prescience sometimes. This doesn't just happen with you. Remember the off the cuff, yeah, you spent the night explaining Kierkegaard to that hot babe...

yeah, yeah, I did! Can't play pool? Ah, yes, the return of comedy. Good. You hit rock bottom and there's only one thing left to do. The punchline.
Sputnik F1-11

From craigstewart@hotmail.com
Fri 31 Dec 1999 at 08:38

You must be psychic or something as I remember accompanying a friend of mine at midnight to Cheapo record store so he could buy the double Pumpkins album.
brewerfan69

From a.a.strang@molextrics.co.uk
Fri 31 Dec 1999 at 08:48

The thing that's good about this is the impression it gives of vast swathes of people seeking out reaaly bad movies to go and see:

'Yeah, but will it be really bad?'

'I'm not sure; you never can be certain, but it did get some terrible reviews.'

'Well, that's reassuring, at least.'

'Wow, that WAS the worst ever. How the hell are they going to top THAT?'

I found this message on a writer's forum on the internet today. Seemed like the usual freaks.

Why do people enter chat room burdening themselves with names like 'The Tonster' and 'Mammal being'? 'FM' for example stands for, if I can remember, 'Furry (or Fuzzy) Monster'. What is with that? OK so you dont want to use your real name out there in the cyber public space, but, Christ, if someone says to you in a bar, do you want to come along to a party and you agree and then they say, hey, what's your name, you say Rowan or Kit or Toni, or even your own name, you dont say 'Sputnik F1-11' FOR CHRIST'S SAKE.

Man, I think I just invented comedy crystal meth there. Got so totally out of control laughing at my own joke I had to get up and leave my desk, then got back and still couldnt stop laughing till I cried.

Obviously it's not that funny, but it just really got to me. Still snorting and giggling as I write this. I'm fucking hysterical, man. I'm out of it.

Was thinking today about the things I don't know about you as a twentysomething American midwestener. Like: what is your relationship to Smashing Pumpkins' double, concept CDs? Did you and your High school buddies wait till midnight outside your local store on their release date? Or did you hate the Goth dudes who loved the Pumpkins? Or did rival gangs of Pumpkins and Nirvana fans roam your streets dancing and singing new Nirvana and Pumpkin inspired lyrics to tunes from Leonard Bernstein's West Side Story?

My two images for American education: elementary
school is like show and tell by Peppermint
Patty, with Marcie saying 'That was good, sir'.
And then the bleachers scene from Grease. 'Tell
me more...' Man that's dumb. Of course, I'm
really thinking, even though you grew up in the
late eighties early nineties, that somehow you
lived through Dazed and Confused singing Pete
Frampton songs. How the hell did that happen?
I was a big fan of Frampton Comes Alive. What a
waste of a lifetime this has all been. Oh man.

From craigstewart@hotmail.com
Fri 31 Dec 1999 at 08:38

I saw Magnolia when I was back home pre-XMAS and
when I saw it loads of people left the theater
and there were many old people there who said to
each other when leaving things like 'that was
the worst movie ever' or just 'worst ever'.

From a.a.strang@molextrics.co.uk
Fri 31 Dec 1999 at 08:46

I told you that story, right? I was on a bus
in Paris surrounded by all these American jock
students and one said he met this girl who was
so dumb he felt he had to ask her, HOW DID YOU
EVER GET TO COLLEGE? And she answered, UH, I
DROVE.

NO. WHO IS JOHN STAMOS?

From craigstewart@hotmail.com
Fri 31 Dec 1999 at 08:38

An American reporter girl I was talking to
last night didn't know the capital of France.
I felt bad for her. Thinking I need to write
a book about being sent on this assignment in
particular, as opposed to my last idea which
was a book about being sent on my last assignment. But my agent only gets me journalism
gigs when I freelance. I need an different
agent for books, I think.

From a.a.strang@molextrics.co.uk
Fri 31 Dec 1999 at 08:45

Chanandler Bong. That was thiss weeks repeat.
Rachael says her favorite movie is Liai-
sons Dangeruese, but it's really Weekend At
Bernie's. Is that the one about the dead guy?
Woooo hoooo! Hello! HELLO! Is this thing on?
I am a great uncle as of yesterday. Sudden
thoughts of how my 21 yr old nephew is some-
how more engaged in life than I can ever be.
Jeez.

From craigstewart@hotmail.com
Fri 31 Dec 1999 at 08:38

My friend who owes me thousands of dollars
hasn't returned my phone calls and I found out
he's vacationing in Jamaica.

From a.a.strang@molextrics.co.uk
Fri 31 Dec 1999 at 08:44

Dude. Get that button on to 'All work and no
play makes Jack a dull boy' and scare your
friends and family. Dig it?

From craigstewart@hotmail.com
Fri 31 Dec 1999 at 08:38

Forgot to tell you that Joe Gould's Secret has
been made into a film with Ian Holm as Joe Gould.
There was a picture of Ian in the NY Times all
dressed up as Joe and the picture was right next
to a picture of Christian Bale as Pat Bateman.
Apparently both films will be at Redford's Sundance
festival.

Synchronicity dude. Sting was right. You will
know synchronicity.
Synchronicity   Synchronicity   Synchronicity
Synchronicity Synchronicity
Synchronicity   Synchronicity   Synchronicity
Synchronicity Synchronicity
Synchronicity   Synchronicity   Synchronicity
Synchronicity Synchronicity
Synchronicity   Synchronicity   Synchronicity
Synchronicity

There's this cool button on the computer that
lets you repeat stuff without typing it over
and over and I've discovered this button and I
am not crazy.

From a.a.strang@molextrics.co.uk
Fri 31 Dec 1999 at 08:43

That guy David Wallace Foster is getting coverage
over here. Hannah has baby. Things happen. World
turns. We work. I standing looking at sky. Nice sky.

From craigstewart@hotmail.com
Fri 31 Dec 1999 at 08:38

I might not send e-mails often, but when I do
they're thick with substance. Was told I look like
John Stamos by drunk girl in bar last Sat night.
Do you know John Stamos in Scotland?

From a.a.strang@molextrics.co.uk
Fri 31 Dec 1999 at 08:42

I find it interesting that we are able to communicate
in a way, across the world and to my very ends of
the earth (though of course you are at the ends
of the earth for me here) in a way that even 15
months ago we couldn't, since oyu got the e-mail
address from The Mole. Go back 15 years and I'm
not even sure phone calls would have been eco-
nomically viable if they had even worked at all.
It might have been those gossamer thin blue air-
mail letters for us, remember the ones we talked
about?, taking a month to get to me here. Maybe
more. I mean I'm out here in the middle of the
Pacific Ocean (are you trying to tell me that the
Pacific Ocean is a greater ocean than the Atlantic
Ocean?!?!), so maybe a month to Aus than another
month to get out to me here.

From craigstewart@hotmail.com
Fri 31 Dec 1999 at 08:38

Director of the FSB. Oh oh.

From a.a.strang@molextrics.co.uk
Fri 31 Dec 1999 at 08:40

Who is this Putin guy?

From craigstewart@hotmail.com
Fri 31 Dec 1999 at 08:38

Looks like Yeltsin has been deposed. Resignation
speech.

From a.a.strang@molextrics.co.uk
Fri 31 Dec 1999 at 08:40

He's had a twenty Prime Ministers. None of them
have lasted.

From craigstewart@hotmail.com
Fri 31 Dec 1999 at 08:38

Er...

From a.a.strang@molextrics.co.uk
Fri 31 Dec 1999 at 08:40

Who's the Prime Minister?

From craigstewart@hotmail.com
Fri 31 Dec 1999 at 08:38

Who'd succeedd him?

From a.a.strang@molextrics.co.uk
Fri 31 Dec 1999 at 08:39

Yeah, dude, legless is what we've all been
hearing about him.

From craigstewart@hotmail.com
Fri 31 Dec 1999 at 08:38

Ha! I don't think he's got a leg to stand on.

From a.a.strang@molextrics.co.uk
Fri 31 Dec 1999 at 08:39

Yeah, history not going to judge kindly, I
fear. Maybe he was pissed off at the criticism
of his dancing and singing?

From craigstewart@hotmail.com
Fri 31 Dec 1999 at 08:38

That would imply some level of competence
from Yeltsin!. Beginning of the end for him,
dude?

From a.a.strang@molextrics.co.uk
Fri 31 Dec 1999 at 08:39

Stroke
of
mid-
night?

From craigstewart@hotmail.com
Fri 31 Dec 1999 at 08:38

Not

strike

of min-

dight?

Strike

of the

clock?

From a.a.strang@molextrics.co.uk
Fri 31 Dec 1999 at 08:39

Adopt the

correct pos-

ture, head

between legs

as far as you

can and kiss

your sweet

ass goodbye.

From craigstewart@hotmail.com
Fri 31 Dec 1999 at 08:38

Yea

h,

wel

com

e t

o t

he

end

of
the
wor
ld.

From a.a.strang@molextrics.co.uk
Fri 31 Dec 1999 at 08:38

HA
!
Th
e
ai
r
st
ri
ke
s
co
me
at
th
e
st
ro
ke
o
f
mi
dn
ig
ht
.

CHAPTER 7

From craigstewart@hotmail.com
Fri 31 Dec 1999 at 08:38

W

e

s

t

a

r

t

b

o

m

b

i

n

g

a

t

m

i

d

n

i

g

h

t

?

J
u
s
t
r

c
h
e
c
k
i
n
g

n
o
w
.

L
o
o
k
i
n
g

a
t

R
e
u
t

CHAPTER 7

e

r

s

.

From a.a.strang@molextrics.co.uk
Fri 31 Dec 1999 at 08:38

I

t

'

s

a

c

t

u

a

l

l

y

a

K

r

e

m

l

i

n

a

n

n
o
u
n
c
e
m
e
n
t
.

From craigstewart@hotmail.com
Fri 31 Dec 1999 at 08:38

H
u
h
?

From a.a.strang@molextrics.co.uk
Fri 31 Dec 1999 at 08:38

W
h
a
t

d
o

R
u
s
s
i
a

CHAPTER 7

h
a
v
e

t
o

s
a
y

a
b
o
u
t

t
h
e

m
i
l
l
e
n
n
i
u
m
?

From craigstewart@hotmail.com
Fri 31 Dec 1999 at 08:38

D
u
d
e
,

g
e
t
t
i
n
g

w
o
r
d

f
r
o
m

A
P

w
i
r
e

t
h
e
r
,
s

g
o
i
n
g

t
o

b
e

a
n

a
n
n
o
u
n
c
e
m
e
n
t

from

Moscow?

You

hearing

anything?

CHAPTER 7

From a.a.strang@molextrics.co.uk
Fri 31 Dec 1999 at 08:38

A
r
e

y
o
u

h
e
a
r
i
n
g

t
h
e

n
e
w
s

f
r
o
m

R
u
s
s
i
a
?

8

15 minutes to go

I'm in the poets' pub, Milne's, at the corner of Hanover Street and Rose Street in the heart of the New Town, that marvel of Georgian ingenuity, the grid system of houses, shops and offices in elegant wide-streeted, pleasantly gardened blocks. From the cacophony of voices, drunkly shouting, someone says there are fifteen minutes to midnight. This is when I start to Billy Pilgrim. Distinctly and clearly it's 1985 and I'm in the Boyd Orr Building, upstairs in a lab for Molecular Biology, the genetics practical element. We're etherising Drosophila that, if our cross-breeding has worked correctly, will have a recognisable pattern of bright red or white eye colour. Then I'm slipping the bottles of ether, from my workbench and a couple of others, into my lab coat pocket, looking out across the rooftops of the West End and completing the action forgetfully. Now it's later that week and we're having an impromptu ether party, after I fess up to my theft of the drug to my flatmates in the flat in West Princes Street. Then it's the next day and one of the flatmates is telling me the upstairs neighbour has just been at the door and she says we can't be having masses of people in the flat for a party, 'not mid-week, please.' There had been three of us, later joined by a fourth, but the ether had made us pretty high and loud. One of the guys in the flat, the Patrick that stayed in the room first on the right as you entered the hall, had been particularly loud, repeatedly screaming that his brain had been turned into a Roland Juno-106 synthesiser somehow: he heard all sounds as though manipulated by the instrument. We had all been kicking up merry hell. Then it's New Year's Eve 1983 and a group of us are at the Pavilion in Ayr for the celebration. I suppose the day must be falling on the night we would usually be there anyway. Back in the now, I'm in the office at Molextrics clicking a left chevron back through the calendar on my laptop and watch the countdown 1999, 1998, 1997, 96, 95, 94, 93, 92, 91, 90, 89, 8, 7, 6, 5, 4, 3. And there is it. 31st December 1983. S. Saturday. So yes, the usual day, the usual night. Then I'm in a Mexican restaurant in the Old Town with three friends in 1997, then in James Thin's bookshop in 1989, stealing a book, *A Thief's Journal*, slipping it in my big coat's humungous inside pocket. I'm scanning the departures board looking for GLASGOW in Euston Station in London in 1987, Ayr in my parents' house's living room just after we moved to Ayr in 1974, on Ayr beach at night in 1992, sitting quietly reading *Slaughterhouse-Five* in the Pandora café in Ayr in 1981... I'm rummaging around the experiences of a life like we all do, every day, every hour, but the re-experiencing is so vivid that I might as well be there. Billy Pilgrim is, I know, but will only find out later, a metaphor for how memory works in later life, mibby especially as you are in the dying days, dying hours, minutes, seconds of that life. Billy had walked in on his own death many times. That awaits for me to find out. And thinking this, and how these are all memories of the past rather than visions of the future, I am walking down a hospital corridor towards a ward. My father has had surgery and I'm visiting him as he recuperates. Except... there seems to be a child walking with me, at least just behind me, and I'm fairly certain this isn't my child. I look towards the daylight coming into the windowless corridor from the ward. This is the old Ayr County Hospital, isn't it? And it's 1994. Isn't it? I'm back at my desk in Molextrics, using Netscape to look up when Ayr County Hospital was demolished and I read it was in 1991. Something's wrong. I'm back in the corridor. The child is still there, just behind me. I'm close to the open ward doors, the daylight I am approaching. I'm frightened.

I'm back in Milne's on New Year's Eve 1999. It's fifteen minutes to midnight. Voices all around me, assailing me, fragments of this conversation here, that conversation there.

Alba, Scotia, Caledonia, Strathclyde—
That still exists.
It's a historical name. Pictland, the Gaeltacht.

Gimme a Glen Froig
Mate, it's a Laphroig.
Yeah, a Laphroig.
Why are you such an asshole?
Give him a break.

The only railway station in the world named after a novel.
Aye, well, named after the English hero of that novel.

T'fuck is *this*?
The music? It's the Pet Shop Boys.
Fuck me. If ye're gonnae play music, play The Eagles. Everybody likes The Eagles. No this shite.

Iain's coming in from North Queensferry. But I think after midnight.
I thought he still lived in Edinburgh.
Mibby he's been out with the parents.

Ken, I've been cooried in fur maist oh the winter so I have. Huv you no?

Aye, me too. Disnae do to be oot an aboot.

Naw, know what you mean.

Ye cannae be opposed to immigration in Scotland, fur fucksake.

Well, it has to be... I mean, the disaster in Sighthill...

Sighthill? And how many desperate people did Edinburgh take in the dispersal, eh?

Well. The same?

Nane. Do you have any fucking idea how many Scots people pissed off round the world from the, I don't know, 1840s to the 1960s? Emigration defined this country. The place emptied of three million people.

Nothing prouder than the clan system.

Oh, aye? Like its version in the States, the Ku Klux Klan?

That had nothing to do with—

Aw naw? The original Klan members, do you know which heritage they came from?

Tell me not the Scots!

'Fraid so, pal. Klan by name, Klan by nature. Neil Oliver says he's going to make a programme on it one day. Says he's got some interest from telly and is going to make loads of programmes.

Seems a wee bit of a stretch, just based on clan and Klan.

Jesus. I never knew.

Aye, and they hoods are fae the Papes!

Are you sure the Klan heritage wusnae Ulster boys?

I just cannae believe it!

Well, you should meet Shuggie the racist from my close!

It strikes me at some point that is difficult to pinpoint within the duration of anything, since time is not passing, that this is not a Heaven-gifted vision I am having but a hell of being unable to move forward through time and hence get to the next moment that is not this one and to some relief from this experience. Am I in hell in Milne's in Edinburgh, moments from − though, again, this construction of words makes little sense − from the − there may be only one word for it − from the beginning − if it is, given the caveats − from the beginning of the second millennium?

Across the road a small group of religious types are shouting in unison, We are waiting for the second coming! Repent! The end is nigh! But then the idea that they are serious religious types dissolves and resolves into the actual reality that they are students, or at least youngish adults shouting ironically.

Caledonian antisyzygy.

The whit?

Where extremes meet. Muir centres it on the inability to both think and feel in the same language.

Yaaass! Ya byootie, mare oh that fur me, feelin great I amn't. And yet, hold on now. Now one comes to think about it, there may be a grain of truth in the sensibility.

Aye, very good.

You an imperial subject now? British Empire?

Roman. Caledonia was the Roman's name for hereabouts. Naw, the tribe, the Caledonii. Something like that.

Well, aye, OK, then.

The American voice saying, *Of Mice and Men* and *The Catcher in the Rye* are quotes from what?

Burns. Sort of quotes. Not Catcher, that's a misquote.

Burns? What's Burns?

Robert Burns.

Ah! Rabbie Burns! Of course. Auld Langzyne! I love it when they sing it at the end of *It's a Wonderful Life.*

Aye.

We asked the Scottish people, Whit the fuck dae ye want? There's the question richt there for you.

Naebuddy wants tae talk aboot politics.

Oh, Flower of Scotland!

Shut it.

Scottish history? No, we didn't really get that. I was at a Catholic school. Most we got was, And then the Reformation happened, ooh, and that was very, very bad…! I had to buy a book on Scottish history when I was in my twenties, find out what the hell had gone on.

Aye, well mibby the Reformation was a particular disaster for Scotland. In England what did it lead to? Shakespeare and the flowering of poetic drama, Shakespeare, Marlowe, Jonson. And what did we get in Scotland. The Satire of the Three Estates and nothing after that. The Calvinists had shut the theatres and stopped all fun.

And who oversaw the English flowering? The King we gave them, James! James! And the beauty of the Bible in English, all sponsored by our James. The King James Bible. The wise old fool. In Scotland he thought it better to hunt witches.

What's your point?

Bannockburn, Culloden, Stirling Bridge, Flodden. Eh?

Poetry.

Caledonia's been everything I've ever had.
Go on, then, sing it.

Here's tae us. Wha's like us?
Gie few and they're aw deid.
I'm sure Beckett would say, Wha's like us? Billions.

It's a braw bricht moonlicht nicht the nicht.
Is it? I hudnae noticed.
Dunno. Jist sayin it.

Heard the one about Connery for king?
Connolly? I'd vote for that.
Connery. You don't get tae vote.
How no?
Naebdy does. No fer a king.

Ha! Aye, that's what it was to be Scottish when we were growing up.
Aye, Hugh… I mean John. John Laurie.
Aye. We're doomed!
Aye.
Dad's Army.
We're dooomed!
We're doooomed!
DOOMED!
He wiz better in *Whisky Galore.*
WE'RE DOOOOOOMED!
AYE! DOOOOOMED!
DOOOOOOOOMED!

Because what the greatest art, the greatest song or painting or film does, right, is stop time.

Stop time.

Aye, something like that. Stop the time around you, anyway. You're not in time any more, you're in the song, or the painting, or the film. You're in the film's time, not in the time around you. Stop time or at least make time move forward in a different way.

Eh?

You mean your dialect. I'd hardly go as far as saying Scots is a language.

Well, that's a political statement that you are allowed to make. But ye're wrang.

Come on. What's the commonality of the words wrong and wrang? Scots is English in a kilt.

I was at a wedding in England last year. Everyone in kilts, all the men, you know. Then there was a ceilidh. I mean, it was fun. But the band kept playing all the dances half time so the caller could lead the English people through them. Try dancing an eightsome reel half time! I kept tripping up!

You Scotch—

Scotch? Scotch? I'm Scots. We're Scots. Get it right.

Oh, I do beg your pardon.

Scotch. Is a whisky. The people of Scotland are Scots or Scottish.

Well, I'm sorry.

Aye. You ur. Very sorry specimen indeed.

Well. There's no need for rudeness.

You think calling people *Scotch* is not rude?

Look, young man, I have said I am sorry. I think we'll leave it at that.

Aye. Well. Get it right.

She walks away towards me and I laugh for many gleeful moments hearing this Betty *sotto voce* saying, Sheesh, what an asshole.

A politician and his special adviser are talking and the politician is saying, Yes, and we've set it structurally so that none of us can ever have a clear majority in the Parliament. We will always dominate, of course. It's the natural order of things in Scotland.

The Overton window you were speaking of to Angus.

Yes, of course, the natural centre ground of Scotland is well and for ever to the left. We will dominate, predominate, if you like.

And of course that's important.

Of course, but not as important as the fact that were we ever to see an ascendency of the Nats, which, no doubt they will gain a little from their current base, devolution has swung that for them, if no more, the idea that the Scots people can be more in charge of their own affairs without the horses taking fright.

They can still never win an overall majority.

Exactly so. Oh, we're clever. Oh so clever.

But doesn't giving them the possibility, remote as it may be, to these—

The Nats. Yes?

Isn't there an inherent possibility we have created a monster in Edinburgh?

Well, you seem to be conjuring a Robert Louis Stevenson romance for yourself.

But the Nats?

Yes, well, the *Nats*. I spell that with a silent G at the start, you know? A-ha a-ha ha ha he he ha ho, you know?

And the laughter falls into a cave, ricocheting off the walls, echoing, becoming distant and then silent.

Aye, the British Empire. Oppressed us for a thousand years.

A thousand? Four hunner, mibby.

Aye, still.

Eh? And, onyway, British Empire was built by Scottish sodgers.

Oh aye. There was a soldier, a Scottish soldier and he was Scottish, and he was a soldier!

These hills are not highland hills, these are my land's hills. Get it right!

Somehow, and I'm not exactly sure how, I'm not here and this isn't happening. I can hear it, and I can see it, but it's like watching and listening to a film, initially. A thunderous actioner, all sound and fury signifying something or other. But it's like there is no it within it. Like there is no itness. No essence of the material reality of it. Like a film: representation not reality. The phenomenon from fifteen days ago, the shell thought, but writ large. Not just people this time, but an emptying of the material from inside all solid bodies to leave only facades. It divided from the very thing that makes it it. Shorn of its itness. Devoid of the very thing inside of it that manifests itself as it to the world. Ephemeral surfaces remain, made of nothing, projections, a virtual universe, a sort of meta universe. The thing as it looks and sounds and smells and feels, not as it *is*.

Nausea. The nausea. Sartre's nausea. Where was my *La Nausée*? Still with Nicola, whom last I leant it to, disappearing into The Grosvenor Cafe in Ruthven Lane, years ago? Or was that other copy of *Ulysses* a sorry for going on to lose it? Going On to Lose It: a Memoir. I snap out of this, but only in so far as I see a woman turn from her friends to a man and I hear her calling out, Oh my *God*, Patrick! What are you doing here?

This Patrick looks kind of stunned, like he wasn't expecting the woman to speak to him.

The thing is, though, is that how I am Billy Pilgrimming is that time isn't moving forward. Like fifteen weeks ago, I'm stuck in the frozen moment. But I can hear and see everything and everyone around me, all at once. So people are saying things and I can hear them, but were you to imagine the sound in front of you, it wouldn't be from left to right, replaced by the next sentence going from left to right, the way subtitles do, but coming at you from directly in front, or from over there, or over there, the way sound comes at us, directly towards us down a tunnel of sound.

A cacophony of words and images that I sit at the centre of, but which I can also separately discern and differentiate. All layered over my own thoughts and feelings and sensations, the speech and movements and gestures of each and every person in Milne's Bar in the New Town in Edinburgh at fifteen minutes to midnight on the 31st of December 1999. A frozen moment. The moment everyone sees what's on the end of everyone's fork, Burroughs' naked lunch become a Scottish pub at New Year Bacchanal. The moment caught in the camera's light's flash. The screams, shouts, faces flushed and contorting with speech, the hands lifted for emphasis, in joy, in placation. The freeze-frame, except with everything moving within the frame, the Brownian motion of the mad moment. And within my bubble of time I can follow down a conversation or watch what's happening for as long or as short a time as I like and it's still fifteen minutes to midnight.

So it's not slowed down or stopped, time, is it? It's looping around, folding upon itself into little spheres of existence, experience, though when they hit me – I can't think of it another way – they unfold and play themselves out, one after another, in a sequence that constructs a pattern of sound, vision, feeling, smelling, experiencing, being aware of, in short, a *reality*.

Susan Alison. More like, wha are you doing here? 'Cause I moved to Edinburgh las year, says this Patrick.

Well, fair enough, as you always used to say. I suppose I am the interloper here. But where else but Edinburgh is there for anyone to be on this occasion? I was just saying to Sam, here... She indicates one of the men she is drinking with. And he was like, Absolutely, the only place to be in the world right now, waiting for the New Year! And I said, The new *millennium*! And he said, Of course! Of course! And now you're here, Patrick. Wow. I haven't seen you in ages.

Well, you wouldn have, would you? Remember, Patrick, stop coming to my house, Susan Alison?

Oh, come on, now. Patrick. You know that had to be said. I was like, Patrick...! Anyway. Who are you with? Come and have a drink with us. Bygones are bygones, aren't they? For auld lang syne, as the man says. Who are you with?

Patrick looks around himself and says, I seem to have temporarily los my compatrios. For the time being.

One of her friends, this Susan Alison's friend, interrupts, gets himself between Susan Alison and this Patrick and shouts, HERE IT COMES! THE END OF THE WORLD!

No, Susan Alison says calmly, I've heard the end of the world and it doesn't sound like this.

OH AYE? WHAT DOES IT SOUND LIKE, THEN? KNOW? her friend shouts.

Well, she says, If you've heard Mogwai doing 'Fear Satan' live – the four guitarists of the Apocalypse, you know? Like that.

I shoo go, Patrick says.

God, you weren't here with Douglas, were you? Oh! Come and have a drink with me and my friends, Patrick! Most of them live in Edinburgh. You might get to know them! Though, you'll be like, It's no that small a town, Susan Alison! Well, you never know!

Listening to these people, Susan Alison and Patrick, speaking, reminds me of my Patrick and the plan to get me through the technical at Mole's. And within my frozen moment I allow myself a wander down a memory from just before getting employed there. Because, the truth is, I know nothing about computers or networks or the Y2K bug, or how I was supposed to fix it. You must have guessed by now. I've been doing nothing during this job. Nothing but the distractions I've been telling you about. That has been all I've been doing. For months now, fifteen months.

The plan for the technical interview was something like what we did for the references I had got for the interview with Molextrics. That is to say, those references were all from so-obscure-you-would-react-WHO?-but-then-not-care-as-they-described-things-no-human-should-know on the technical skills of Patrick, that semi-autistic computer geek, with his computer skills also going into the forgery of these references into my name. And the plan was a doozy and probably owed much of its infrastructure to Patrick overdosing on *Mission Impossible* in 1996. He was the one who came up with the overall idea: me; a wireless earpiece; a new short-range wireless technology, which was going to be called RadioWire or PAN (for 'Personal Area Networking') but which had taken off under a placeholder brand name of 'Bluetooth'; a mobile phone; another mobile phone; a microphone and Patrick at the end of this chain. And Patrick's technical knowledge of all things specifically networky, softwarey and generally computery.

Why wasn't Patrick himself just going for the job? Three reasons. Patrick doesn't like the real world, doesn't like people, doesn't want to leave his room much, doesn't want to stop gaming. He's a real Lawnmower Man, happiest in *la réalité virtuelle*. Two. Patrick's minimal engagement with real life means he has minimal needs, minimal outgoings and therefore, what with a few other circumstances that I'll leave private to Patrick, he didn't need the money. And last, Patrick didn't believe for one minute, one second, one nanosecond, that anything was going to go wrong with computers at the millennium, as the year ticked over from 99 to 00. Now, said Patrick, if there had been computers and software developed in 1900, we might have had a problem. And I said, Good! So, they're offering this money, this *huge* amount of money, and all I have to do is go in there like I know something, make it look like I'm out of my tits working my bollocks off for the next fifteen months doing… *something*, and the fact is I don't have to do *anything*? Patrick, this is the job I was made for, the one my whole background and experience have been leading towards! The only thing is, how do I convince them to give me the job in the first place? I'll have to show them I know *something*.

Interesting, Patrick said. Tell, me, do you know anything about eschatology?

It's a religious thing, I said.

Very specific.

Well…

It's the study of the Christian theology of last things, Patrick says. Part of that is millenniumism, that somehow on millennial dates something big, the end of the world mostly, but all the other last things will come to pass, Second Coming of Jesus, the Rapture, the Tribulation, the new Heaven and Earth, the coming of the Kingdom of God, the resurrection of the dead, all that.

OK.

So, you don't think that this belief in these cataclysms around the millennium would mibby affect how people feel about this millennium?

I get your point.

And millenniumism is even more pervasive than just in Christianity, or even in religion itself.

Mmm.

Oh yeah, and also in eschatology there's the Last Judgement, when we'll all have to account for our sins.

Yeah? So? I can tell you're trying to say something else.

Well, do you think you'd be able to convince the ultimate judge that what you're about to do with regard to Mole and the Y2K bug is something you can defend?

Yeah, the thing is, Patrick, is the Last Judgement coming?

No, but the point remains.

It's just a job, Patrick.

I mean, I wasn't completely ignorant. I just didn't know *enough*. No one did about this millennium bug. No one *knew*. This was my downfall *and* my salvation.

This Susan Alison and Patrick that I'm watching and listening to are still talking, and he hasn't quite joined her and her friends, but he has looked around them.

Douglas isn't with you, then? he says.

You know, I don't think I've seen him this year. I don't actually think I saw him last year, either. Have you?

This year? Or last? I don think so, no.

No. New York seems to keep a pretty firm hold of him! To be honest, Patrick, I think the last time I saw him I said something like, You're no artist. You're a drunk who gets work in galleries. And he was like—

Ouch, says this Patrick. You can be fuckin brutal when you choose, Suse.

I'll take that as a compliment, shall I, Patrick?

If you like.

Well, I don't know what that means, but I'll let it pass. Oh, come on and have a drink with my friends. We're all just in here, in Little Kremlin.

My Patrick set to work making the suitable Bluetooth-enabled earpiece and Bluetooth-enabled mobile phone by adapting this and that and making other thises and thats from scratch. The only time Patrick really likes operating in the real world is when he could make or amend this or that. Patrick has a brain the size of a planet. And, you may ask, why do I have privileged access in reality to Patrick's attention? No special reason. Something to do with his hair and getting him to look up from his book. It's between me and him, really. We go way back, Patrick and me.

Does this plan look hare-brained to you? And, I suppose more importantly, did it look hare-brained to me? Well, yes and no. Bluetooth had only just been invented. Would audio that could be heard by me also leak into the room? We had tried using the earpiece a few times in the days up to the presentation part of the interview, the 'how did we get to the millennium?' part I started this story off with, but had not yet got past a need for me to rustle about and clear my throat or continually say, Mhmm, mhmm, mhmm, as though I was acknowledging the question but for a weirdly prolonged time when Patrick was speaking to me to cover his voice in my ear. A deadly silent room was going to be exactly that, deadly, unless, in the couple of days we had left before the technical interview, we came up with a better solution. I was going to be left looking like a nut.

This Susan Alison says, Well, anyway, Douglas was like, Aye, that sounds like the naked truth. We always spoke to each other that way. And we could take the truth from each other. We still can.

I think he was thinking it was the nake truth in a different way to the way you're thinking, Susan Alison.

What? What do you mean? He was saying… He said, This is OK, I can take the… the—

He was saying that he knew you inside and out, and that you could take him and tear him up into tiny wee pieces if you chose to. Tha's wha he was saying.

No! You're wrong! Oh, anyway, what does it matter? Patrick, this is my husband, Jonathan.

Hi, Patrick, says this Jonathan, and reaches to shake his hand.

Patrick nods. I better get back to looking for my…

Jonathan reaches his hand to Patrick's shoulder and taps twice. Nice to meet you, fella.

Yes, well. It was nice to see you, Patrick, Susan Alison says.

This Patrick moves away from the group of people, pushing his way through the throng.

Who was that? this Jonathan says to his wife. I make the decision to go past them and towards Patrick.

Patrrick… McCoy?

The real Mc—

No, McCabe! Or McCoy. Oh, I can't remember. Though, honestly? she says as I pass. Nobody.

I follow this Patrick for a moment, towards the door, and as he starts to ascend to the street. Patrick, who is shaking his head, is saying to himself, She'll kill him one of these days.

I stand for a moment, watching this Patrick I've been listening to and watching as he ascends the stairs up to street level and wanders north towards George Street, where there's a Bank of Scotland ATM with a short queue of people waiting to take money out. A man at the head of the queue seems to be getting pretty exercised about his transaction, keeping turning and shouting at the people in the queue behind him.

It's sayin it's no gonnae! he says, apparently referring to the cash machine. Is that it, aye? he's shouting at the machine now, going through the motions of another withdrawal, apparently. I want the fuckin lot cleared! He shouts back at the queue. Youse'll huvtae wait. I want the lot. Fuckin banks are goin tae fail at midnight.

Naw they're no! someone in the queue says to him.

AYE THEY UR, shouts the man. Don't you lot know anythin? Y2K! Y2K! The banks are gonnae fail!

They hud people in for aw that, likesay, another person in the queue says.

Those fuckin eejits? Everybuddy knows they did fuck all, know? says the man at the cash machine. He's thumping buttons on the keyboard. I'm getting as much oot as I can, anyway.

Well, fuckin get it and let us get oors. Fer fuck's sake. Jambo.

It's only fuckin lettin me get two hunner at a time, ken! And now it's telling me I cannae get any mare! Fuckin piece of shit! He thumps his fist down on the keyboard.

Oi, for fuck's sake, man, if you break that I'll break you! I need more money for drink! If you were that bothered about it, why didn't you get it out slowly over the last few weeks?

Thirty-first hud tae be a Friday, dinnit? I didnae get paid till the day.

But what took you to close to midnight—

That's when I knew the bank system was fuckin up, din't I? Fuckin wages never came through till aboot hauf an oor ago!

Heh, he's right, mine took ages too the night.

It's the fuckin millennium New Year, it's just overloaded.

You think?

Aye. The millennium bug is a hoax! If the end of the fuckin world was all hinged on the millennium bug, why would that affect your wages goin in before midnight?

I don't trust it now, either, I want all my money out now.

It's probably nutters like you pulling all their cash out because of worldwide hysteria that the banks are so slow. No other country has reported the millennium bug doing anything.

So fucking what? It's no midnight yet!

Well, numpty, it's been midnight all over the world before it gets to midnight here. Haven't you ever seen the fireworks from Sydney Harbour?

Aye, but that's no the real New Year's, is it? This is. The one in Edinburgh. GMT, likesay.

What?! Are you an idiot? It's been New Year over most of the earth already. Are you some kind of flat-earth nutter?

Stop calling me a nutter, right?

I didn't call you a nutter.

Aye, ye did.

Naw, I never.

Look, just get out the fuckin way and let the rest of us get oor money if it won't give you any mare, eh?

I walk back down the stairs into Milne's and to the back bar, where I stand next to a couple of men at the counter who, before I hear what they are actually talking about, I watch them gesticulate and get drinks in for themselves and two women sitting further back in the bar at a crowded table of other people who they do not seem to be with. Then I hear one of the women calling over and asking what time it is and how long they have and one of the men checks his watch and says to the other, Tell them it's quarter to, Paul, fifteen minutes to go, and this man Paul flashes ten fingers then five at the women and one of the women nods.

So I'm still in this time-anomaly bubble, where it is staying quarter to midnight but also I seem able to follow conversations and scenes as they move through time. Or mibby I'm just mistaken and it hasn't been quarter to until now, or mibby these people are wrong about the time and it's actually ten or five to midnight, or both them and I are wrong, it hasn't been quarter to for me before now and it isn't quarter to for any of us now. It's the way this cellar pub has become an insanely loud and flashing scene, people, drinks, shouting, spillages. I'm thinking of how my mind read the title of Jeff Torrington's *The Devil's Carousel* as *The Devil's Carousal* for the first year or so that it was out. This scene in Milne's is both a carousal and a carousel. My stomach lurches for a second on the carousing carousel.

I turn to lean on the counter for the stability it affords and I hear Paul telling the other man, Of course, logically and figuratively, Scotland is a fiction, built on a fiction, on fictions. Clans, the purely Scots fighting men fighting the purely English invaders.

You mean, like, were Scots colonised or colonisers?

Exactly. Once the English were colonised, when the Scots couldn't be, under the Romans. Do you hear us going on and on about oh pity us, we were colonised by the Romans? Nope. We rose up as English and—

Yeah, right, went marauding round the world building a brutal empire for ourselves instead.

Yeah!

Of course the answer is both, but they and we choose our times to see ourselves as one or the other, the colonisers or the colonised. But, of course, for the Scots all they always talk about is the glorious defeat. God, we love losing more than we love winning, because there is more honour in that.

You saying you're Scots, now, Paul?

Oh, aye. Scots parents mean Scots git, Patrick.

What, another one? How many Patricks are drinking in here tonight? Haven't seen this many Paddies since they worked on the railways!

Tenuous, mate, tenuous, says this Patrick. The way you say oh aye doesn't even sound right. Sounds like the way… Well, sounds like the way I say oh aye.

What the hell was that? Mate, you're not a Geordie!

Wey, aye, canny lad!

Fuck me. Stop, mate.

A huge man turns to them, having overheard what I've overheard.

Now, gentlemen, he says. Please be careful, this conversation may be heard by a less gentle giant than myself.

Paul and Patrick turn to the man, looking up at the six foot six of him.

We Scots, he says, are speakers of a language that is not our own, somehow, and yet we are experts in this language. Has not the English language been developed in parallel in England and Scotland for hundreds of years? The ancestors of the people who bemoan the taking of the Gaelic from us were unlikely to have ever been speaking a recognisable form of it, even at the time of the rosy-golden period sometime when. God, even English from then would have been absolutely unrecognisable to us. Have you tried to read Chaucer? Beowulf? Have you any idea how many English neologisms came into usage because of the Scottish Enlightenment? An enlightenment built on the free flow of debate in that most useful and flexible of modern European languages, English! Clans, kilts, shortbread. Capitalism. The dollar speaks and Edinburgh and all of Scotland listen. Talk about sell your granny! A myth, myths upon myths, the not-a-mile-long Royal Mile—

It's an abandoned measure's mile long, a good Scots mile! Patrick says.

Paul turns from the man mountain and looks at Patrick. I read it, today, on the Royal Mile. A plaque, Patrick says and shrugs.

I will not be shouted down! And what is good about it? That it was Scots, yes, but that it is gone, lost, defeated!

By the English, you mean, no doubt! Paul says. I'm not English!

He's mock jock— I mean mock Scots. Born in England.

That Scots mile was defeated! First, by the Scottish Parliament, twenty odd years before the Act of Union! the gigantic man says. Finally by international pressure and standardisation around the world – don't you know how many miles an hour you are doing for how many miles in the States, Canada, South Africa, Australia, New Zealand?

Ah! The English colonies!

British colonies, jam-packed with descendants of Scots! A nation! Brigadoon in the mist! An ephemera. A ghost, a ghoul! A nation. In name only, so what is the point?

Too harsh an analysis.

You think? What's yours?

Oh, now, I'm not saying you're wrong.

Paul turns back to the counter of the bar, hunches his shoulders, then turns back to the large man. Have a good night, mate, he says, then turns back to hunching on the bar. Patrick joins him in the same posture.

So, this Patrick says, how does it feel to be institutionally racist?

Shh, Paul says, not here, not now. Not ever, in fact.

Who knows us here?

That's not the point. We start talking about it when we feel comfortable that we're anonymous, we end up saying it at the wrong time and in the wrong place.

How's it going with you, anyway? I mean, now you have a kid? We can talk about that, can't we? We can talk about how you feel about having a girlfriend who's now the mother of your kid?

Well, I mean, it was a bit of an unforeseen. The boss might not see it that way, though.

What, they've commented?

No comment.

From them, or is that from you?

No comment. Not without my brief present. And keep up with your front on you being a carpenter, OK?

OK, that's fair. So, this friend of Julia's. What's the story?

What? You wanting a bit of domestic bliss, too?

Nah, mate. I believe what I'm looking for in this city is called my hole.

Nice. Paul turns to face the two women. Ah, fuck. You're probably right with that aim. I tell you, once the home's set up and the kid's in the way and the woman starts getting fucking fat. A right little fatso she was just a while back.

Patrick glances around at the women, then back at Paul.

She lost the beef again, thank fuck, says Paul. If she'd stayed a fatso I'd definitely have been off to the funny farm.

Focus, mate, Patrick says. This discussion is not getting me my hole. The friend?

I don't know her, she's just someone that lives here that Julia knows. One of her old uni pals. One of her oldest pals, in fact.

Yeah, mate, but she lives alone as far as I could make out earlier when we all arrived.

Well, the mother was there to look after Liv tonight, wasn't she?

She said she was heading back to her own place when we got back. So. What's her name again?

Olivia. That's why Liv's called Olivia, too. Like I say, one of Julia's oldest pals.

Into drugs at all?

You aren't holding, are you?

This Patrick smiles, straightens up and gets into position to order another round.

Jesus, Patrick, Paul says. You're unbelievable.

So, this Olivia? Up for it?

She's one of those ones. All her boyfriends have been shits, no doubt, so she sees women and misogyny as the only two issues in the world. You know the type. If only women ruled the world, though Thatcher was a witch. If only inventions by women were more recognised, except they haven't invented anything. Well, maybe the ironing board or something. But what's happened throughout history is us men have just ignored what an important contribution women have made to... something. She has all these books, you know, women who discovered things, were explorers. Artist women who haven't had their due. Stuff like that.

Is that right?

I tell you one she won't have, though. No book about all the women who were holy terrors. Irma Grese, Bloody Mary, Isabella of Castile. Look them up, mate. Aileen Wuornos, Myra was as bad as Brady, Rosemary West was as bad as Fred. Beverley Allitt. Maybe men have ignored women in all sorts of ways, but they've also ignored how fucking awful they can be. I'm writing that book, I think. Forgotten women who were utterly abysmal. I'll title it *Cunts*.

So, this Olivia? Is she or is she not up for it?

What have I just told you?

They're the ones I like. Liberated women, mate.

You'll need to ask her, mate. Fucking between you two.

Yeah, that's what I was hoping, too.

154

I walk over and sit next to this Julia and Olivia, who don't notice because of the general rabblement and mad shouting and drinking going on around us. They don't even notice when I move in close to be able to hear them talking. They both look up, over to the counter where Paul and Patrick are standing and Paul makes the ten and five fingers gesture again, to which one of the women nods, which gives me the impression that this one is Julia, Paul's partner. It also tells me that again, time has not passed, and we somehow remain at a quarter to midnight.

For a second, a microsecond, a nanosecond, it strikes me that this time thing cannot possibly be true in any real sense, and that therefore all this that seems to be happening around me is in fact not. That I am experiencing something, but not the real world, not in real life. But what is it then, if not that? Because it feels real, it feels real to me, anyway. It looks real and it sounds real. But the laws of the universe, the laws of physics, beloved for being unchangeable for that fake Scot, Mr Scott of the *USS Enterprise*, are not being adhered to. We're in a world of the broken laws of physics. Things flit through my head. A game. They've become so elaborate, these immersive worlds. The holodeck on the *Enterprise* of *The Next Generation*. The simulation of the universe that keeps being speculated upon. I think again that what I am having is more simply a poetic vision of Scotland, rather than an experience of an actual Scotland. But, like the big man was telling this Paul and Patrick, even that Scotland is a fiction in and of itself. Especially tonight of all nights it's the shortbread-tin image of itself, like it was at the opening of the Scottish Parliament by the Queen, when the full mock jockery of it was in full swing. It comes to me that for the first time I make the connection and realise the lack of connection between Jarry's syzygy and MacDiarmid's antisyzygy, while also realising I could not fully explain this were I asked without being very drunk indeed! Is it the drink that is providing me with the vision around me, the things I am seeing and hearing and smelling and feeling around me? If so, it must be the drunkest I have ever managed to be – but I don't remember drinking that much, and certainly not more than I have ever drunk before. But then is that an effect of the amount of drink I have had, being unable to measure how much I have drunk? Have I had consciousness blanks or black-outs during which I have continued to drink more and drink recklessly, mezcal or absinthe or somesuch, which have caused these… this vision?

Now what is striking me is that what the spatial and temporal phenomenon I am experiencing, my time bubble, my ability to move from place to place at will without constraint of apparent corporeality, what with the crowd seeming to part as I make my way anywhere, may mean is that, of course and obviously, I'm dead. I look down at my hand. No spectral transparency there, however. I hold the hand up to the light. Nope, just a hand, just *my* hand: I am aware of it from the inside as well as viewing it from the outside. I snap my finger. All seems in order, nothing unusual at all. And I don't 'come to' with the snap, as though I have been hypnotised or self-hypnotised and this snapping finger is what will make me snap out of this state. And I suppose the lack of being spectral, the lack of transparency of any sort, kind of leaves me with the fact of my corporeality. But why does the crowd *part* as I pass through it? I consider for a moment I am part of that biblical other demographic, some cherubim or seraphim, an angel or a devil, one of those Heavenly Host creatures. Mm. Seems unlikely.

I decide I cannot know, not now nor here, so I'll pass the not-passing time listening to this Julia and Olivia. I lean in to listen. They do seem eminently unaware of my presence. Perhaps I am a ghost. Can you be a ghost when you don't believe in ghosts? I guess if you're reading these words after I've died, I'm a ghost of a sort. That kind of ghost I do believe in.

Tell me about it, Olivia says.

I'm not sure I can, Julia replies. It is quite painful.

To say?

To even just think about. She pauses. I just didn't ever think this would be me, you know? I know we all grow up at some point, but not even having Liv made me feel like I feel just now.

And how is that?

I feel... I feel old for the first time. An adult for the first time.

I think I know what you mean.

Yeah? We all go through things. When your dad died...

That made me feel curiously young, like I'd become his wee girl again. Maybe the thought is, I'm too young to have a parent who is dead. Grandparents, fine, but parent? It's all happening... too fast. Life is passing too fast.

Yup, I know that feeling.

Yeah. Yup, I know that feelin.

You do it better. So, that's how I felt, too, now you say it. Like I was too young for this to have happened.

You felt too young and too old simultaneously? Yeah, that works for me. Maybe that is how I felt as well, when my dad died. Old with the responsibility that I had to look after my mum now.

You felt straight away it was for you to look after her as opposed to her look after you?

Yeah, you're right. It was straight away. She looked so frail at the funeral. I mean, it had started before that with the two of them. You know, like the first time you see your parent get fankled with a piece of perfectly simple new technology?

Oh God, yeah. The first time I saw my dad try to work the Underground ticket barrier. Think I was still a student then, and he just couldn't put a piece of cardboard through a slot. Thing was, I'd just gone ahead through the barrier next to his and on to the escalator down. It wasn't till I turned round and he was calling me, Julia! Julia! But it didn't seem right to try and make my way backwards back up to him on the down escalator. As I stood there helpless, the person behind him got pissed off and did it for him.

Parents. They're a worry.

Yeah, that old one.

So, it made you feel old. But why did you... I mean, what happened before that?

Before that? Before that. Before that I knew what I was going to do as soon as I found out.

Just like that?

Yeah, just like that. Knew straight away. Liv was three, would turn four. I just couldn't see it happening. It all seemed... oh, I don't know, the wrong thing. The wrong thing at the wrong time.

Well, I suppose you have to think that way. I mean, anyone has to think that way. You've got to know that it's the right thing at the right time, don't you.

Well...

I mean, with Liv, didn't you feel it was the right thing at the right time?

Well...

OK. Maybe there never is a right time, or a right thing.

It was partly to do with... Oh, I don't know, I don't know what it was partly to do with. All I knew was that with me and Paul, and now Liv, it was making things... It was making things super-complicated. I mean, my head was like… And this Julia makes a gesture, like she is shaking her head to aneurysm between her hands.

Yeah, says Olivia. With a wee one around…

It wasn't that. It wasn't that we had Liv. That was just… something that was the way it was. What could we do about it? And it had been wrong timing. Very wrong timing.

Yeah, but you can never say Liv's the wrong thing, not your daughter.

Julia pauses. No… no, of course not, she says.

Olivia looks up and over at Paul and Patrick hunched over the bar counter. Did you get much information about… anything?

Julia looks across at Paul too. Not much, she says. I mean, what can you know?

And when did you, you know?

Just after the second scan.

The second scan? That's… I thought you said you knew straight away what you were going to do?

I did. But I just didn't… I kept thinking, Maybe this one won't keep going, something would happen, it would go, you know, wrong. I think I convinced myself it would go wrong.

Patrick walks over with two fresh drinks. Ladies, he says.

What time is it? How much longer? Julia says.

About quarter of an hour, this Patrick says.

OK.

Patrick goes back to the bar counter, pushing in to retake up his position next to Paul. The place is even more rammed than it has been, so things are somehow changing within this apparently unchanging time. Or mibby the unchanging size of the crowd is unevenly redistributing itself within this time.

The second scan. That's twenty-two weeks.

I know. Actually I got mine at twenty-one weeks. Just a scheduling thing.

But terminations are only...

I know. When it came down to the actual decision, it had to be made as a kind of snap decision. I only had a couple of weeks to decide.

Oh God.

I knew I was going to do it. I don't know why I waited.

Oh God. It must have been awful for you.

Awful would have been to have had another with him. They both look over at Paul. I mean, says Julia, not awful because it is him. I just mean wrong thing and wrong timing for him more than me.

And you had your twenty-two-week scan. That's when they usually tell you the sex of the baby... if you want to know it.

I told them I didn't want to know.

Probably wise.

But I could see on the scan. This woman called Julia looks about herself, but not actually focusing on anything in particular. It was a boy.

Oh God, Julia, I'm so sorry.

Sorry?

Sorry about what you had to go through. And what did he say about all of it?

Him? He thought I was getting a bit fat and then I lost some weight. She, this Julia, stares into her drink. I didn't tell him. He never knew. She swallows her drink down.

Eventually I stand, finish my drink, which seems to be working out just dandy for me, drinking, so that side of corporeal is fine, and make my way out past the Little Kremlin room to the bottom of the stairs to the street, outside.

I walk to the top of the stairs and see three men walking along Rose Street and into Hanover Street, walking past the entrance down into Milne's and standing at the railings on Hanover Street that run along in front of the pub. I walk back down the stairs to the area below street level in front of the pub and move along through a crowd that again parts for me without fuss, till I'm a couple of feet below the railings on Hanover Street where the three men are standing talking. I know I want to hear what they are saying, because one of them, the one sporting famous hair – I don't know where famous people go to get their hair cut, but it's not somewhere the rest of us are privy to – salt and pepper with a fly-away cut that is simultaneously wild and controlled, is definitely Douglas MacDougal, the famed, perhaps infamous, Douglas MacDougal, and he is standing upstairs from Milne's, and I hear him say, I was at this party once, years back now, and this woman told me that Burns was a drunk, a fornicator and a wastrel, so why are we supposed to admire him as our national poet when he was this drunk, you know, this fornicator and this wastrel? Those were her actual words. I didn't say to her, you know, but her description made me interested in Burns for the first time in my life, Andy.

Ah, I see! says this wee Andy. My generation spent all our time trying to make him respectable, so that we could admire him, accept him and separate him for all the sexism and misogyny, for example. And we ended up with…

Aye? Aye. For most of my life, Burns has been the strangulated asexuality of 'My Love Is Like a Red, Red Rose' sung by Kenneth McKellar, with strings and harp accompaniment. Bloody awful. Anglicised pronunciation of Scots words. Till aw…ll the seas gang dryyyyy…! Jesus Christ! Brigadoon! My generation wanted – and wants – rock'n'rollers.

Aye, weel, that's you noo, is it not? The rock-and-roll artist!
Guess so.

A person walking past turns to Douglas, this wee Andy and
the other man, who is not famous and I don't know, and says,
Are you Douglas MacDougal?

No, he's a much less handsome, shorter guy. A bit fat.
Beard, glasses. Looks older than me. Like that guy down
there, he says, nodding – I have no idea why, as I look nothing
like what he's describing, the opposite, in fact – at me, not
realising I can hear everything separately at once.

Come on, Douglas. You are Douglas, says the new person.
Aye, fair enough.

Everyone loves looking at your art.

Do they? Cannae be many of them. Most of it's stored,
gathering investment payback.

It's as I'm standing here at the door that I start to think
that this is some kind of Edinburgh show, being staged in
front of me. A theatre piece being enacted with each stage
direction and monologue and dialogue written, somewhere, and that I am the audience for the performance. Or
I'm the director? It just seems... rehearsed. A scene played
out in a million, a billion places tonight. The rowdy pub,
the jubilant New Year's Eve party-goers, over-lubricated.
In Milne's in Edinburgh, the Café Royal, the Oxford,
the Barony... in Edinburgh, in Glasgow, Aberdeen, Ayr,
Kirkcudbright, Kirkintilloch, Bonnybridge, Sollas...
in London, Copenhagen, Helsinki, Paris, New York,
Berlin, Moscow, Delhi, Sydney, Ko Pha Nga, Tokyo...
Los Angeles, Chicago, in Milwaukee and in Denver... in
Cumnock, Maybole, Skares, Auchinleck, Muirkirk... But
this one is the one I am the audience for, except people
keep looking to me, especially when they have fluffed or
are fluffing their lines. So I may well be the director of

this play. I turn and actually I know that I am. I am the director of this play.

I wish I could disappear from view even more, but you probably need me here, don't you, leading you through the highways and byways? So, thinking logically, I'm the ghost at the party, I'm Banquo, the deus ex machina. Or... You're a gamer gaming. The shell people from before they are avatars and your shelllike self was and is your avatar. You're in the game right now and the packets of time and experience are game scenarios you've been through one, two, a million times, repeating the same place and time but varying the experience. It's almost too obvious, so obvious that it can't possibly be right, can't possibly be real. Not you. I mean me. I'm a gamer gaming. Except, as I say, I'm not.

I remember there was a day I was sitting in the car of a girlfriend – I was visiting her in Carlisle, where she lived – and I had a library book I had just started reading while I waited for her as she ran some errand or other. When she got back in the car and I looked up from the page I said, Wow, that was a while. I seemed to have read my way through close on fifty pages of the book, a strange Oulipo or nouveau roman novel in which time didn't seem to move forward. What are you talking about? she said, I was about five minutes. It was something about sitting in the car quietly, with Carlisle town moving about its business around me, outside, that had mibby skewed my perspective, my experience of phenomenological time, my time-consciousness. For a moment, as we sat there and the girlfriend prepared to drive away from where we were parked, to return to her house in Lorne Crescent, her first bought house, I thought about a lab assistant for the Genetics element of my Molecular Biology classes talking about the phenomenological experience of time of

Drosophila, that these fruit flies live for about eighty to one hundred days, at the end of which they are extremely old and knackered, and how he guessed they must experience a passing minute as – he did a quick calculation: 80 days x 24 hours x 60 minutes = 115,200 minutes of life for fruit fly; 80 years x 365 days x 24 hours x 60 minutes = 42,048,000 minutes for human; 365 ÷ 60 = 6ish – so six hours of human phenomenological time. When we talked about it later, his calculating seemed to go round the houses a bit, but he was working out the logic of it, I guess. This isn't the point of this story. The point is, I have returned many times to think and replay this scene of sitting in the car waiting so many times. Countless times. And now I sometimes think that the time I had sitting there reading a novel where time didn't move forward, my experience of it as a very long time indeed, is somehow – how? – all those moments of thinking about it in retrospect being crushed back up into the past is what produced that extra phenomenological time I experienced. As I say, how? It just seems to fit together like that for me, illogical as it is. Mibby. Mibby fits. Mibby everyone has experiences like this. I think they do, anyway. I can't remember what the actual novel was now. There's a few possibles. Those French writers loved all that playing-with-time patter.

This is when it strikes me that, were I to typewrite these experiences the way I have been experiencing them, here in Milne's Bar, in New Town, in Edinburgh, in Scotland tonight, at a quarter or so to midnight (GMT) on the night of the 31st of December 1999 into the 1st of January 2000, old-style, ink roll and mechanically typed, with a DING at the end of a sentence, and a return but then frequently with an added double-clunking anticlockwise twist of the platen knob, moving the platen and with it the paper back two lines, then for typing to recommence, would just become these black splodges of text, hundreds of them, written one on top of the other, until it looked something like:

And also that they, these little packages of always fifteen minutes to midnight, are like the thousand flaring embers of the fireworks that were about to go off, in fifteen minutes or so.

9

15 seconds to go

In the frozen moment, the scene has changed and I'm in the Café Royal bar, West Register Street – which is still in Edinburgh if you don't know Edinburgh – but still I'm thinking that if I was or were manually typing down what I could hear and see it would look like this:

The sound in my ears now is like the tippy-tapping the main character hears in Muriel Spark's debut novel *The Comforters*, that infernal tip tip tip tap tap tap. But the typewriter carriage is moving less from side to side before the carriage release lever is swished and the platen knob is twisted back so that the typing actually looks like this:

The sound now is furious, like the electric typewriter teleprinter punching the paper at the end of *All the President's Men*, but like the mechanism is stuck, neither moving to the side nor down because time is slowing down and slowing down until we get to:

Although time is not yet completely slowed to a stop, because that, in manual or electric typewriting terms, or even word processing, would look like this:

That is, nothing on the page at all. But because we are at the stage before this last stage, it's just that time is now balled up into a dense sphere of ink splodge, or rather, represented by a dense splodgy spot, and I realise that these folded lines of linear experience are related to quanta of spacetime and what that means is that perhaps I am sitting outside the three dimensions of space, the four dimensions including the dimension of time, in one of the further dimensions that quantum physicists now suspect or speculate there are. Or mibby I'm outside all the dimensions, but then how would I be able to think, were I outside them all? Possibly it's one of those everything is everything thoughts and if you think anything is outside this everything, it's not, it just adds to what everything is. So that if I'm somewhere outside, say, ten dimensions, that's just an eleventh dimension, or if I think I'm outside the twenty-six dimensions, then I'm just in the twenty-seventh.

The nothing on the page like the last fizzle out of the last firework to come. A dark sky.

When I'm within the four dimensions of normal space and time, around me the more sober, restauranty, sedate caution of the Café Royal is being thrown to the wind and all is similar to the tumult and chaos and cacophony of Milne's. People are shouting, laughing, screaming in each other's ears. The crowd is packed in and seems to sway as one at certain points of both time and space. Someone smashes a glass and a round of cries and applause goes up and circles the ceiling corners of the room.

It's fifteen seconds to midnight, and over at a booth, where a group of friends are drinking and cheersing each other, *Slainte! Slainte! Slainte!*, there are two people standing, part of and apart from the group. One looks like Jean Cocteau, who did have a tendency to look like an old Scots gentleman of his era, with a similar shock of hair to, say, a rural doctor or a farmer, or a dominie of some school or other, mibby even like Hugh MacDiarmid's. The other person looks like Dame Commander of the Order of the British Empire Muriel Spark – in other words a Scottish woman of her age, height, in that she is tiny, now if not previously, and features that look seen-it-all kindly. I suppose it could be Dame Muriel Spark, as she is still alive, unlike Jean Cocteau, though she never leaves Italy these days. But, I suppose, she might have – left Italy, that is – for an event such as the millennium in Edinburgh, where she was born and schooled and, as she has it, 'formed'. But, no, she does not look quite enough like Muriel Spark, or not consistently enough as she moves and speaks and laughs and drinks, just as Jean Cocteau keeps changing in the light and as the crowd moves, so that sometimes he's very Jean Cocteau and at others he's not much Jean Cocteau at all.

I'm moving through the crowd, though slowly, as the place is so densely packed, with an outstretched arm doing the magic trick of parting the crowd as I go, and I notice I am holding a glass of something, spirit, wine or beer, I can't exactly see which, can't even see if it is a wine or pint or spirit glass, there's just too much noise, too many people, too much movement to concentrate on what's in my hand. It is only a bulwark to get me through the crowd. I'm headed over to Cocteau and Spark. Cocteau is throwing back his head at something Spark has said and I want to be in on their joke, their conversation.

As I draw closer I can hear them speaking, and as soon as I am able to hear them it strikes me that these people could actually be Jean Cocteau and Muriel Spark. The Cocteau man – let's establish him as this for the time being, even though 'time being' is a fairly fluid concept for us at the moment, as is 'at the moment', as is 'us', I suppose – is talking about his presence in the National Galleries of Scotland, and the Museums of Scotland in Edinburgh. So, I suppose this man is an artist, like Cocteau. With quite a thing for looking like Cocteau, you'd have to say. Well, to each their own. But then he starts talking about his long association with the Edinburgh International Festival, so I start thinking, artist, writer, playwright, theatre director... He could be any of these things. They're not so unusual in Edinburgh, in the Café Royal, which is quite the hoity-toity howf, it has to be said. But then the Muriel Spark lady, who is looking very Muriel Spark just at the minute, it has to be said, asks what the association is exactly. She has rarely been near the festival, what with her travels to London and New York and now Italy, a strange coincidence since these have been the places where the actual Dame Muriel Spark has lived her life.

169

It's dawning on me slowly, I suspect more slowly than it is for you, that, of course, this is actually Dame Muriel Spark, here in the Café Royal in Edinburgh at fifteen seconds to midnight on the millennium. How extraordinary! I'm feeling pleased with myself that I have 'bagged' what must surely be one of the most superb accidental meetings in Edinburgh tonight. So many people will just miss seeing this or that celebrity, actor, comedian, musician, pop star, artist, artiste or poet, or even just this or that person they know or a politician, one of the old stagers like Alex Salmond, Henry McLeish, Donald Dewar, Margaret Ewing or Jack McConnell, or one of the new faces like Tommy Sheridan, Fiona Hyslop, Pauline McNeill or Nicola Sturgeon, the future of Scottish politics looking very like a production of Ibsen's *The Master Builder* from this perspective, tonight in this packed Edinburgh pub with fifteen seconds to go till midnight. Dame Muriel Spark! I feel like shouting. I cannot… I'm just so…

I wonder who the Jean Cocteau is, now. Some eminent Scots man of letters? Some friend here with her from Tuscany? He could so equally be from Italy as Scotland. Remember, I come from the west coast, from Ayr; half the kids in my school were of Italian descent, mostly from Barga in Tuscany, so…

Then the Jean Cocteau answers Dame Muriel's question to him, and he says, My association with the Edinburgh International Festival was deep and illustrious. I designed the covers for the programmes on a number of occasions.

But, I'm thinking, so did Jean Cocteau! I hold my drink to my lips – and it's a glass of white wine, by the way, I can see now – but when I drink I feel queasy. Or is it unease? Too many coincidences strain belief and make me deeply disconcerted, and I'm still not absolutely going with what is happening, even though I know that time has gone weird.

Then I accept, as you probably have a paragraph or two back in the telling. This *is* Jean Cocteau, even though just at the moment he bears a resemblance to Jack McConnell, while Muriel Spark looks uncannily like Nicola Sturgeon, just from this angle, in this light, a younger Muriel Spark looking like an older Nicola Sturgeon, somehow. Then Jean Cocteau laughs uproariously, looking straight at me, and I get the uncanny sense that he's not laughing at something Muriel Spark has said, but actually at *me*, my dull-headed slow realisation of who he and his companion are, and he goes through a rapid succession of looking, sounding and moving like, and, I have a feeling, *being* Paul Buchanan, Robert Louis Stevenson, John Byrne, James Kelman, then back to being Jean Cocteau. Muriel Spark lifts her glass to toast the fifteen seconds to go until it's midnight and she *is*, in rapid succession, Elspeth Barker, Jenni Calder, Elizabeth Fraser then Lena Zavaroni. Then she is Muriel Spark again.

I have the distinct feeling that not the physical body but rather the spirit, the consciousness or imagination, of Dame Muriel Spark is what or who I am now standing beside. It's something to do with the instability of personality I am witnessing, or, more precisely, experiencing: I *know* that these people, Jean Cocteau, who is dead, and Muriel Spark, who is almost certainly in Tuscany and not here in Edinburgh, in the sense she's not there but here, who can also become other people when, it seems, they emote or move too quickly, forcefully, are the essences of who these people are or were, but not them. Above all else, as will soon be seen, their individualities and personalities, *them*, in fact, *they* are unstable. But then so is the differentiation of 'will be seen', 'having been seen' and 'seeing' itself unstable.

This is when it strikes me, what with a lightning storm of thoughts striking in the same place not just twice, but repetitively and frequently, that Dame Muriel Spark being here in some form, body or spirit or something, and the way I am moving and seeing and hearing and experiencing, is giving me an indication of who I might be, or, rather, what I might be. Because Spark is famed for her omniscient narrators, the all-knowing of her writing, and who the all-knower is. Because her fiction is lauded, no matter what it seems to be on the surface, as being a discussion about God, with the all-knower being this God character, conflated with the all-knowing writer, Dame Muriel herself, she and God standing above and around and beneath all the characters at all times understanding everything. Well, with regard to me being this kind of narrator, I suppose it's a theory. Mibby I'm here because Spark has summoned me, and it's not I who has summoned her.

I can hear them perfectly now I am standing right beside them, and Jean Cocteau is telling Dame Muriel that, after his death in 1963, he decided to travel more, that he had barely ever been anywhere outside France, and he wanted to make his home in a variety of places, including in Scotland. He took up residence in a number of galleries and museums in Scotland, in houses and in libraries, and has stayed in a number of different theatres, both stage and cinema, in Scotland in the years since his death. Oh, yes, says Dame Muriel, I also like to travel, but not *physically*. Not now. It's all too much bother! I'm too old. And she laughs, strangely – because strange is now the opposite of what is usually strange – remaining herself throughout her knowing, gentle laugh.

Which is all to say, this is probably why Jean Cocteau and Dame Muriel Spark are standing in the Café Royal now, with fifteen seconds to go until midnight on the 31st of December 1999 into the 1st of January 2000.

Does transmission of image still occur nowadays? Cocteau asks.

Oh yes, says Spark. Television, cinema… A film was made of my Jean Brodie, and a television series. And there is something to do with computers that I'm too old to take an interest in.

Ah! says Cocteau. I thought as much. See, I dinnae believe in death. But I'm still seen by people, eh? A ghostly presence on television and in cinema still.

Why Cocteau has a Scots accent I'm not really sure.

Don't believe in death? Spark says. Yes, I can see why. Or the end of the world?

Certainement pas! Cocteau says. His accent is Scottish even when he is speaking French.

Of course, the end of the world had happened by the time I was born, says Spark. The First World War. And, after the end of the world, I was witness to slow death. Was it worse to die quickly in the war or to survive? They came home to nothing. And the small boy selling newspapers at the Toll Cross with nary shirt nor vest under his paper-thin jacket, barefoot in the cold of a winter's night. The slow death of the world's people, particularised in this small boy.

Death, Cocteau says, nodding sagely. Int it jist one of the forms of life? I mean, look at Saint Augustine. Great saint! Do you think he could be all wrang?

One of the greatest. Without a doubt, Spark says.

It's now that something feels like it is about to take flight. Something within me. My consciousness? My imagination? My heart is thumping like it is going to explode through my chest. My blood pressure must be 200 over 140 and my heart rate must be up around 200. Is it possible that it is my soul, our souls, that are about to take flight, flying around the Café Royal now?

Cocteau is saying, Ifin we try to live by watches and clock, diaries and calendar, that's no going to work, now, is it? I will tell you this, what we did was we misled oorselves in oor time, or perhaps these lot are still misleading theirselves in their time.

Oh, very much the latter, Jean. I don't know that there has been any progress on that front.

The way Spark says Jean is sometimes closest to John and sometimes closest to Sean.

Aye, progress. You know, sometimes I think o' progress as the long-time development o' a big, big mistake, you know? Long ago, during the First World War, I went to see Gabriel Voisin's workshop, you know, the major airplane manufacturer. I looked at his airplanes and said, Voisin, how come yer latest airplanes seem the most old-fashioned to me?

I'm assuming that Cocteau now is baring a remarkable resemblance to this Gabriel Voisin. I'm not sure what Voisin looks like, but Cocteau is certainly looking younger, and he has a bushy moustache which is jet black.

Voisin answered: Simple! Made a mistake, din't we? We started wae the wings. It's likesay we made a fuckin car wae legs insteeda wheels! Well, there you go, eh? Laughable. Heh, I'm wondering if they've invented a, you know, some sort of anti-gravitation vehicle by now? Tell me they huv, goan.

Oh! Dame Muriel exclaims, How utterly *delicious*!

Saint Augustine was not wrong, Cocteau continues, There's nae upside down. Burkhard Heim says something along the lines that we'll no fly but fall, and he may well be proved right oan the money.

I feel your reference points may be a little beyond my ken, Jean. Or perhaps I have forgotten much of what I learned that was useless to me at the James Gillespie's High School for Girls. Perhaps, most awful to contemplate of all, my own prime is now years behind me and has fallen away.

Spark pronounces Girls the same way Maggie Smith as Jean Brodie in the film of her book does. With a vowel shift, hardest of gs and an unrolled r: *Gels*. As she speaks she looks for a second like a thirtyish Edinburgh teacher in the 1930s who I suspect to be Christina Kay, then for a split second – should such a thing exist within no time at all – a somewhat comedic, nightcapped man, with a snuff-addict's oedemic nose, whom I take to be James Gillespie.

Cocteau drawls on, Mibby they've discovered or invented some material or other that seems heavy but at the same time is in fact very light thit then escapes gravitation and thit, instead o' rising falls, eh, cuz anti-gravitation involves falling instead o' rising, know what I mean, *ma petite chérie*?

Eh? I'm not sure that's quite how it works, Jean, my dear, but I am too polite to contradict such a fine talker as yourself.

Oh, I'm sure, I dinnae know what is going on in this time, do I, but I think mibby young'uns urnae straddling contradictions like what we did. When we were young we were straddling contradictions. *Vive la révolution* an aw that, great times, heroic times, oot and aboot in Montparnasse, know what I mean? The way it was then, all of us in soapy bubble, *pour encourager les autres* an aw that.

Cocteau goes through rapid changes, appearing as men, women and children, I suspect from a 1920s Montparnasse street or café scene.

Some senses, we're aw jist robots, Cocteau goes on, returning to being himself. I hope these people in these times hinny become robots. Rather, humanised. That's the hope, anyway. But I dinnae ken who people know theseadays or whit they're thinking, let alone whit they're doin, whit dances they're dancing, know? The dance o' ma time was called the twist. Mibby you've heard of it?

You are forgetting my age, Jean! I twisted many nights away, especially when I was at *The New Yorker*!

And these people, most certainly they have their own dance. Or dances.

I think the latter. I wouldn't know.

When I wis livin on the Côte d'Azur there wis Nice, Cannes, Saint-Tropez, Jean-les-pains…

Cocteau is looking like his socialite patron Francine Weisweiller, the other woman, other, that is, than Piaf, who may have hurried his death, they say, from heartbreak. And now Cocteau is looking like a very sad Piaf.

Mais bien sûr! he cries, Soon as ye got aff the beaten track, well, *vraiment magnifique!* Unsullied by the sort of architectural Esperanto that wis my time's big fuckin mistake. Mibby these lot huvnae made the same mistake, eh? Know what I mean, Muriel?

He looks round appreciatively at the internal architecture of the Café Royal, which bears a resemblance to a *grand café* of the Parisian left bank.

Architectural Esparanto? Spark says.

Architectural Esperanto, aye. Nae thought to climate, nur atmospheric conditions nur landscape nur nuthin. I hope that's been binned. Hope they now hiv houses that stir the soul, eh? No prison blocks, barracks.

Oh, Jean, Dame Muriel says sadly, I think you may be disappointed.

This's when I realise, the over-talkative Cocteau is directing this play, this Edinburgh International Festival play that these characters, Cocteau and Spark and I and the people, secondary characters, that they become as they talk about them, are playing out… or in. The thought overwhelms me. At present, we are hovering in front of a window with a Robin Hoodesque bowman in one window and a kilted gamekeeper-type who seems to have just shot a calf or cow, whose head lies at the foot of the image of the gamekeeper with his shotgun. It would be a good stage set and *coup de théâtre* for us to appear to be hovering this way over the heads of the drinkers as they drink and shout and laugh at fifteen second to midnight on this big night.

Telt ye, din't I, me an ma lot, when we were young we straddled contradictions, aye? We kinda loast oor humanity, went roboty. The young, I say to them, Ye're iways too sad an worried, cheer up for fuck's sake. *Mais c'est normal*. Here. You must still ken Picasso, *oui*?

Cocteau grows rotund, bald, shirtless, tanned, black-eyed, staring, being, as he is, the older Picasso.

Picasso says to me, It takes a long time tae grow young, Cocteau says.

How delicious! *C'est magnifique!* Spark says.

The young, ken, dinnae know which way's up, likesay. What's what: *à gauche ou à droite*. Bein worried's bein old, but then ye find yer way. Wance ye stoap wae the hitch-hiking along in life, know?

Cocteau resembles a number of French-looking young adults – an agglomeration of half-remembered actors from Godard and Truffaut movies – hitch-hiker types.

I tell you this, Muriel. Ye think you're getting along jist fine, but ye're no. It's no you getting along fine, it's the driver ye're hitching with, that driver's getting along jist fine. You're jist along for the ride, goin nowhere because you'd be stuck at the side o' the road waeoot the driver's car, the driver's destination. Dae ye see what I mean? Onyways, mibby these days it's aw anti-gravitation cars, vehicles, whathuvye, floating along the road. I'm still haudin oot for the idea these huv been inventit.

Oh, Jean, you are a card! Dame Muriel says, and touches his arm. My only hope these days is to sit down with a James Thin legal pad and write one more book.

Je suis sérieux! The Incas knew all about the secret of anti-gravitation! This secret is lost, but, mibby this lot are, I willnae say sitting, cuz young'uns should never be sitting aboot, they should be go go go, you know? But, mibby they huvnae a clue, not a Scooby Doo, where nur fur whit nur fur why they're headin in the direction they're headin.

I think they may have more of an idea than you credit them with, Jean. There are myths and myths.

Aye. See me, I've iways preferred mythology tae history, Cocteau says, because history, ye see, is a bunch ay truths which eventually turn oot to be lies, whilst the old mythology is a bunch ay lies that eventually come out true, become truths. I mean, ifin I hae the guid fortune to live on in all minds, surely it wid be in the mythological form, ken?

Well, Dame Muriel says, turning to me for the first time, then back to Cocteau. You are with us now! We can see that.

I will tell you why, Cocteau says.

Oh, go on, then, Spark says waspishly.

What's a poet?

Ah, Jean! Now you are asking.

Poet, painter, musician, sculptor, architect or whoever it might be. What's poetical and what's poetry? An I mean poetry as a kinda superior mathematics and, let us not forget, it's almost iways prophetical. That's jist the truth. Each poet a sorta prophet…

Yes, often a prophet without honour in their own land…

And we are very humble about this because a poet is a man…

Or woman, Jean, or woman… Spark says. Anyone.

Yes, yes. A man *or* a woman who resembles those people in the Salpêtrière Hospital.

Cocteau in turn rapidly resembles many people in the Salpêtrière Hospital.

These very ordinary people who say the most extraordinary things under hypnosis. The poet is jist the work-hand of the self, that very self that jist disnae know too well the completely mysterious forces inside the self. Poetry has to be the conduit between *l'intérieur et l'extérieur* and they, the poets, try to make it liveable.

If they can, Jean, if they can.

Exactly what a poet is, Muriel. I'm a character that I'm not, a character fae legend who's jist no at all like me, but who protects me in some way, cuz I wouldnae want this character to shake ma haun, but at the same time he protects me, you know what I mean? Same as the way Don Juan disguises his servant so's the servant gets the beatings that were meant for him, ken, Don Juan.

Cocteau goes through changes to look first like Don Juan, his servant, the man about to beat the servant, Don Juan again.

It's no me what's getting beaten up and burned alive in Burns Statue Square or on the Edinburgh Castle Esplanade. The poet, the inner me, is timeless as a character an I keep well away. I'm no responsible for onythin, I'm no responsible for ma poems. I'm jist the work-hand. All us poets are jist mediums an work-hands for these mysterious forces inside us. *Non?*

Yes, says Dame Muriel, I will not disagree.

It's somethin that comes up from the depths, from oor night, and a poet tries to lay out his night upon the table.

Or *her* night. I do wish you'd—

Yes, yes, I keep tryin tae remember. And he sometimes clumsily helps this deeper me who's usually in a bad mood because he isnae weel served, as they say. Aye, it's me who speaks to you now, fae ma mooth, but poorly, since I'm jist no that me.

Cocteau begins to extremely rapidly become all the characters he has been up to now again.

Look, from oor births to oor deaths we are a stream of others. We're iways another. When I wis in wan o' my wilder moodies I built this church on the beach at Villefranche-sur-Mer then shut maself inside it fur two years.

Cocteau grows into the body of Alasdair Gray, and is speaking in Gray's extraordinary way, whooping and rollercoastering from high to low pitch, high to low register, bouncing from Scots to English and back again.

I painted it… LIKE A PHARAOH painted his *ane* coffin. I was, and this is why I can tell you without shame, already DEAD when I painted this church because I wasn't, so to speak, *quite aw there*. I was simply. A. Worker. Climbing. Ladders… getting on to scaffolding and fixtures. Making a ceiling poses GREAT DIFFICULTIES – I even wonder how Michelangelo managed to do the Sistine Chapel. MHA!

Cocteau has become Michelangelo. The pub goes dark and silent and we see as candlelight illuminates the ceiling, which is half painted à la Sistine Chapel.

Speaking softly, almost whispering, Cocteau says, He'd one candle fixed on his forehead with a wire and this candle must have dripped on him, burning and stinging his face. He didn't paint using what is called tempera paint, he painted *frescoes* – in other words, he was more of a workman than an artist.

Cocteau has become Alasdair Gray again.

AT THIS MOMENT a manual labourer is speaking to *you*. Evidently it happens tae me when I write, not exactly being a manual labourer, since my head and hands must work at the same time, ma hauns serve the Mysterious Person That Lives

In Me and that I MHA, MHA, MHA! don't know. I often
take a rest by doing plastic creation, which means that I often
paint walls. I'm often asked why I paint churches.

Cocteau has now become Ricky Demarco.

It's because I need walls, and I don't find them elsewhere,
except in a building that perhaps no longer exists, and that
was in my day the wedding hall of Menton, which isn't
a church. Generally, I need these walls to GET SOME
REST.

Ricky Demarco and Alasdair Gray are now alternating,
now merging, now separate people.

People tend to think that I get awfy tired: NO, BECAUSE
MY HANDS ARE DOING THE WORK. They become
intelligent. Genius. Oh, ye think I shouldnae be using such a
BIG word? Wrong: one thinks that the word genius is not
to be used and that genius only belongs – Cocteau becomes
Johann Wolfgang von Goethe, Victor Hugo, William
Shakespeare – to Goethe, Hugo, Shakespeare. NUT, NO!
Genius can be the way a woman steps out of her car.

Cocteau is now Stendhal, Marie-Henri Beyle, about age sixty.

Stendhal said a woman could get out of her carriage
with genius. Genius is a kind of superior expression of the
individual. Well, anyway, back to poetry.

Oh, yes please, please do! Dame Spark says.

Ma poems, sich headscratchers when I wis alive, left a load
o' readers and critics flummoxt. Mibby these young people
get them, you know? If I'm still bein read, it goes withoot
sayin. I seemed to be speaking an unknown language.

Poetry should always be written in unknown language,
Spark says. Unknown until the poem is written, and then the
language is known. *For the first time*.

Yes. Yes. Yes. *C'est vrai*. You're a poet. Unknown because it
has to be learned. Jeez, people imagine that you open a book,

181

you look at it, and then you've read it. You haven't! First you need to learn the mysterious language of poetry. I think there is a chance that this language will come down to you while other things that seem more important will not.

I think that's what I said, Jean, only using fewer words. I like economy in all things.

We live in a time obsessed with actuality – immediacy, haste and actuality – and poetry is, I repeat, timeless. That means it jist doesnae match what's happening, it's out-of-the-moment: poetry as a kinda superior mathematics, a supreme language, the man of real genius, the poet, and the poet in all his—

Or her, Jean, Spark says wearily.

—forms is alone. Or her, she is alone. I only hope genius husnae become somethin like a shameful and contagious sickness against which you'd wish to be immunised. Individual genius gets replaced by a great collective and scientific genius, but I say that science, even though it consists of a number of men—

Jean!

—or women, or men *and* women, who come thegither to achieve marvels like the electronic brain, for example, well, at the start of it all there is always a lone man... or woman... who discovers, who invents, and is almost always, by the way, forgotten. And, then again, there's religion.

Now we are heading on to my subject, Jean. You may even let me say more!

Many extraordinary inventions have been stopped deid by religion.

Cocteau now resembles a cardinal in full regalia – Cardinal Tisson, it will become apparent.

There was this first airplane, you know, to leave the ground, before the king and queen of Portugal or somewhere, but, since it was inconceivable to enter the sky without meeting God and the angels, well, religion put a stop to it. Cardinal Tisson told me that the sketches still exist, in Rome, in the Vatican. They are still with us, many extraordinary things have been made centuries ago, but the secrets are lost to us. Example, right? The Ark of the Covenant, the way it's described in the Bible, in acacia tree an negative gold; well, that's actually an electric battery that was made.

Cocteau now looks and sounds like Aminadab of the verses in Exodus (6:14–28), then a cowherd of the time.

This is the reason why, when the Ark is lifted to Aminadab's house, a cowherd that touched it was struck down: it was a battery! This was forgotten, lost and then found again, Muriel.

You're rambling, Jean. I wouldn't mention it but that I feel friendly towards you. Now, I am thinking of my girlhood way back when in this very city. Everything changed many times, but one of those changes was when Penguin paperback reprints started coming out in 1935. Why, a hardback book was seven or eight shillings, whereas these paperback pocket books were first sixpence, and later on ninepence. Can you imagine? I read Maurois and Hemingway. But the greatest of these editions that year was Eric Linklater's *Poet's Pub*. That was the one that expressed and described a world nearest to mine, with a liberated humour and throwaway quality I loved.

I know Maurois. And Hemingway.

Quite. Another published that year was Mary Webb's *Gone to Earth*.

Another favourite?

No. It left me cold, quite dry-eyed. And it was written partly in rustic country dialect, which I loathe in all writing. I won't have it, simply.

Oh aye?

Quite. I much preferred the awfully malicious parody of Webb, Stella Gibbons' *Cold Comfort Farm*. Much more my kind of thing. Malice, and Webb deserved it. Her tosh was written during the First World War – can you imagine? How frivolous! Have you read it? *Cold Comfort Farm*, I mean.

Non.

Oh, you should.

I sincerely hope that mibby war is gone now, eh? And that these mysterious wars called cold wars, which may be even more terrible and dangerous, are gone.

Well…

Many people think that one can stick to old-fashioned politics, other people look too far ahead and lose all sense of reality.

And well… again. I think we are way past that stage.

I am thinking, I love this Spark spirit. She has a greater sense of herself than Cocteau. Though Cocteau has the greater propensity or perhaps capability to transform. Perhaps he is just less sure he is who he is than Spark is that she is Spark. For now, he becomes transparent for a time.

The really remarkable man should be invisible. And if he is given a prize, if he is awarded the *Légion d'honneur*, if he is elected to the Academy… I am a member of the French Academy, the Belgian Academy, the American Academy, the German Academy.

Now, now, Jean. Modesty. Modesty. I am still a woman from Edinburgh, for God's sake!

I am also doctor *honoris causa* at Oxford even though I hardly speak a word of English.

But you seem to be…

Cocteau does seem to be speaking perfectly acceptable Scots-English.

We show ourselves, jist a wee bit. It's probably a mistake. You know about Ravel?

Cocteau is transformed into being Joseph Maurice Ravel.

Ravel gave comical titles to his compositions, Cocteau says. And he refused the *Légion d'honneur*. He said, What matters isnae simply refusing the *Légion d'honneur*. Even more, you shouldnae even deserve it! Of coorse, Satie said of Ravel, Ah yes, sure he refuses the *Légion d'honneur*, but aw his work accepts it! The *Légion d'honneur*, hm. Any chance these frills and flounces have disappeared from art and this lot are now a serious and attentive generation?

Well, I have to say no, Jean.

I see. *Mais bien sûr*, I wish people could keep me in mind – me as the countless others I have been, the mysterious others that inhabit me. I don't want to be remembered as the self speaking to you, but as the self who is in the shadows, my shadows, and who has been expressing himself without control, because, I repeat, control is a dangerous thing and errors, errors are what're the real expression of the individual.

Yes, Dame Muriel Spark says. I will accede to this.

Cocteau yet again becomes Pablo Ruiz Picasso, though this time as a serious young man.

Cuz if Picasso puts an eye where it shouldnae be, ye see it all the more clearly than if he'd placed it where it should be. A settee in a sitting room is in the right place, so's it's invisible; but put out on the street it becomes a settee all over again! Art has an element of surprise, more than science. I mean...

Cocteau becomes Descartes.

It's clear that all that Descartes said jist dusnae add up, right? Yet Descartes remains Descartes because he's a great writer.

Cocteau becomes Cocteau.

In reality, ma work shows ye who I am, mare than the me you see right in front of you right the noo. And if ma work's worthwhile, well, I want tae huv written on my gravestone: I'm startin oot.

Oh, delicious, yet again! Dame Muriel Spark says. Well said. I will have on my gravestone: *Poeta*.

I am in the Café Royal, Edinburgh, and I feel there is something about my... soul, my perception of everything at once, the feeling I know everything at this moment... I feel I am about to take flight. And it's as though, if I were some novelist, I'm trying to write a state-of-the-nation novel, a statement of Where Scotland is NOW or something, because I can conceive of this moment and this place, see it all and hear it all, everything that is important now. Is this a vision? I sound drugged but I'm only drunk, like the whole of Scotland's population, in its cities and towns and villages and farms and countryside, everyone is drunk. And I am looking at a thistled nation. And what I hear and see is:

What do you think? Will Scotland want to go independent, or will it want to stay a part of England in the future?

Mate, it's those kind of statements that probably tell you why independence is becoming a hot topic here.

You know what I mean, part of the UK, of Britain.

Well, you said what you said.

In the future, we'll ask ourselves, where were you on the millennium? Well, I'm right here. Here I am. The only living boy in New Town.

You know when she dies, if he keeps his name, he'll become Charles the Third. Now, this is to remind us of the great river of heredity that flows down through the years, decades, centuries of a royal family, right?

I suppose.

Aye, that's what it's for. So, with the name thing, we're reminded of Charles the Second, right?

Sure. You get a third, you're wondering who the last one was.

And do you know who Charles the Second was?

Go on.

He's the monarch in the seventeen hundreds who formed the Royal Africa Company, which would eventually become the largest slave company in the world. He formed it with his brother, James, who acceded to the throne after his brother. Scoundrels, both.

Come on, now, you can't blame the descendants for the crimes of the ancestors.

I'm not doing that, I'm saying what is monarchy for, if not reminding us that God, almighty God, makes these people our sovereign because of the special quality they have, part of which is who they are born of? The chain links up through history to these other special, God-chosen people. What I'm saying, that he'll be Charles the Third, is specifically to remind us there was a Charles the Second, and a first, giving the third legitimacy. And I'm just telling you what we'll be reminded of in reality.

Wasn't Charles the First the one who was executed? Cromwell and the English Civil War and the republic. Always well forgotten, that, in the supposed unending chain of monarchs.

Well, Charles the Second was his living son at the Restoration, had been on the run in Europe for most of the time.

Aye, but no the king.

Well, he was the king of somewhere. I'm not sure I want to say it.

Where?

Well, after his faither had his heid lopped off, the Covenanter Parliament of Scotland proclaimed him Charles the Second of Scotland.

That was politics.

Aye, it always is politics. And look what happened. Charles stuffed the Covenanters eventually and the last four years of his life reigned as an absolute… well, I was going to use a word there, but the right word is monarch, absolute monarch.

They're all as bad as each other.

Aye, but you can choose a new name as your king name, can't you? He'll do that, because he'll realise what you have realised. That's what they do. They're smart that way.

Mibby. Mibby they'll be that cynical.

We are talking the royal family, here. Cynical doesn't cover it. They're ruthless.

Aye, it's Shakespearean. Dripping in blood.

Aye, and the Scottish monarchy was worst for that, according to Shakespeare. The Scottish play. I saw a production of that once at the Tron, and it was blood everywhere.

And when Charlie-boy gets his billions fae his mum, they'll be the billions he has because Charles the Second built that company and sold those slaves.

Aye, I see your point now. He'll change it, won't he?

If he's as smart and ruthless as his mother, aye.

D'ye know what song played publicly in Edinburgh on the occasions of the Union in 1707?

What? Which?

They played 'How Can I Be Sad on This My Wedding Day?' Over the rooftops of Edinburgh. They played it slow and sad.

Over the rooftops, was it? Wee bit of poetic licence, that.
Aye, well, MacDiarmid said every Scot was a poet.
Pish.

I'm talking about history, a shared history, and the character of the nation, our identity! Our nation!

Well, let me tell you. Character is a fiction. Identity is a fiction. Chronology is a fiction. In here. Even fiction is a fiction. And a tautology is a tautology is a tautology is a tautology and smells of nothing. Ah, but a rose! A rose still smells sweet!

Look, what I'm askin is, how would you vote if there wiz a vote?

Let's see. I am a Scot, born in Glasgow. Fair enough. But it means nothing. I live in England now. Cambridge. I don't get to have a say, franchise-wise. I try to therefore not have an opinion.

Come on, you must have an opinion on the fate of your nation. Your home.

My home in Cambridge is quite nice, thanks. But as to home, a Somali who's been living in Sighthill for the last six weeks, ever since they arrived in Scotland, has more right to say what they would vote than I do. I don't live in Scotland.

So you don't care?

On Burns Night and St Andrew's day I fly a Saltire flag outside the bedroom window of my house. It's just some local colour. Like a Chinese New Year celebration in Chinatown in Soho. You know?

It strikes me now that, as I laid out how we got to here, or, rather, got to now in my talk to the Molextrics people, at that presentation which feels like a million years ago now, I could put together a future to match the past. 150 years after – the centenary celebration all over the nation of

Scottish Independence – 1,500 years after – exhausted yet hopeful after years of war between European states during the Fifteenth World War, Scotland joins with England, Ireland and Wales in integrating into the European superstate, Europa, the parliament of which begins debates on abating the huge decline in populations worldwide – 15,000 years after – the world government makes initial plans for the escape of human consciousness from a dying planet – 150,000 years after – the decline of human so-called 'IRL' civilisation and the fleet of sealed vessels seeding post-life human consciousness into space, which is, in the end, a hastily assembled affair as curating what 'human consciousness' was proved too divisive and ended as a bundling-together the sum total of just everything that was on the web pages of all those sites we know so well, which will, no doubt, take over the world – 1,500,000 years after – the final end of the earth as a planet which sustains life – 15 million years after – the dispersal of human consciousness vessels far into deep space, where no other consciousness or life is discovered – 150 million years after – all functions of the human consciousness vessels finally fail – 1 billion 500 million years after – an enlarging sun expands out towards the inner planets, turning all of them molten – 15 billion years after – the last moments of the dying sun and the end of the solar system – 150 billion years after – the nothingness of before the beginning: again, in no time there was nothing nowhere. I mean nothing everywhere. Although, if there is nothing wherever where is, then it's unlikely, to say the least, that there will be many wheres making up every one of them. Seems more likely there would be none. None wheres. No wheres. No theres. No heres, theres nor everywheres. Or anywheres. This is just semantics now. No ises, no ares, no wases, no weres.

This is how the world ends. Let's roll back from 150 billion years after right now to now. I mean, it is New Year, so it is the time for a bit of despair, but I don't want you thinking in terms of utter despair, staring into the nothing, the dark silence. We'll save that for another time.

Back in the cacophony of the Café Royal, it strikes me that the people around me are definitely... here – I'm not sure... here because I am here? Here because of me? Where they are all over the city, all over the world, tonight. That somehow it's all because I perceive them that they are here, in front of me, acting the way they are because, again somehow, in some act of volition, I will it. It feels really peculiarly like I am making them all act and say and do what I will them to, like I am directing them in a play, or a film, that the way they appear to me is the way I am making them appear to me. Or like I'm writing the film or the play they are in and simultaneously they are able to know how to act, what to do and say because I have written these things, stage directions, dialogue, for them. I'm not going to lie. I am in a panic. It's disconcerting, feeling this way, feeling it so strongly. As if I am the writer, and these are just characters, characters I have written. Like I am writing a novel and everything that is happening around me is the plot and the characters have the characteristics I have written for them and say the things I have written.

One character says, Did you hear what he says he wants in the new millennium? Ian? Ian, did you hear what he says he wants?

And the other character is saying, I heard him, aye, some idea!

And a character I am making appear laughing at the bar says, Aye, Rex Scottorum, he wants Sean Connery to be our king!

Then the first character says, Well, if we make it into the new millennium, I suppose anything could happen.

And the second says, Aye, all bets are aff!

Laughter. I'm making them laugh at each other's comments.

We're no making it, by your reckoning? I make a character continue.

It's why his pals all went to Uist, you know? They thought when the bug hit… I have the first character say, because I have written the script this way, the dialogue in the novel.

Aye, lights out.

Lights out! Onyhing could happen.

The end of the world is… nay, man, nay, man… nigh! says this character, though this is a little confusing, because I'm writing this piece of dialogue and yet I'm not wholly, not 100% sure what the character means or why the character I am writing is saying what's being said exactly this way.

Aw aye. Right, likesay, I have another character say.

You lot know nuthin, I make a new character butt in and say, then make her continue, The next end of the world will be right along after this one, don't you worry.

Aye? Yeah, but what will it be? one of the first characters says because I have written this.

The new character says, because I want her to, I don't know. Terrorists will start flying planes into buildings. The climate going nuts. Financial collapse. A virus, a new pox. A war.

There's always wars, I have another character say, and immediately wonder whether I should rewrite this as, There're always wars?

I mean a war where we thought war was all done, I have another character say.

In Europe?

Aye, sure. Yeah, like that. Water wars. Oil wars. Food wars. Clashes of ideology. There's loads of options. Constant surveillance. Controlling us. Algorithms fucking us over…

I mean, I know it's not true – it's not true that I am writing these words or have written these words previously and now these characters are reciting these words. But it feels like that. My mind is battling with my mind. I know these are real people, but the thought won't lift that I am writing them. Again the voices have become fragmentary:

Cuin a bhios sinn neo-eisimeileach bho na luchd-labhairt Beurla seo? I have a character say. The reply is terse.
Seadh.

I'm writing – though I know I'm not, these are real events, real people, I am here in the Café Royal in Edinburgh on millennium night – voices in the tumult, which I am *hearing*, seeing the people *speaking*, coming at me from here, there, over there. Then I hear this dialogue, voices of these characters in here, discussing the different versions of Prince's song '1999':

I was thinking of the big production job and the bossa nova of the Mike Flowers Pops version.

No, come on, the original Prince.

I heard Big Audio Dynamite did a version live.

I'd like to hear that.

Yeah, and Gary Numan.

Have you heard the amazing Dump version? Done as a drone thing. They do all Prince songs as drone things. Pretty cool. An album called *That Skinny Motherfucker with the High Voice?* – ends with a question mark, like you're asking: Prince, that skinny motherfucker with the high voice? *That* Prince?

Classic.

Genius, man.

It comes off kind of sad, which is a good thing. Yeah, but the best sad version of the song…

Sad? Why would you want a party song sad?

Aw, man, I end up sad every fucking New Year.

Aye? Aye, I guess so.

So what was the sad version?

Eh? Oh, P.M. Dawn. It's a medley they play with '1999' in it, called 'Fantasia's Confidential Ghetto'.

What the hell does that mean?

No idea.

Elsewhere, a character is setting a challenge:

I can prove to you that English is a Scots language.

Go on, then, Einstein.

What's the most precise language we ever speak in, write in? Communicate in?

Eh… I don't know. The law? Contracts and stuff.

Very good, yeah, legal language. And what's the legal language of Scotland?

English, I suppose.

Aha! Yes! But now. What kind of law is the law of Scotland? Obviously Scottish law, we have a separate legal system. So, what the person is communicating, in this English, is Scots law, is it not?

Go on.

So if it's expressing precise Scots things, in this language, is it not Scots?

I can sort of—

It is, this English, expressing a Scottish thought, expressed, in, lest we forget, this English that is Scots.

That's not proven.

I begin wondering whether this is a thought I'm having, and giving expression to it through these characters pure and simple. That they are not saying these things, I am thinking them, thinking of them as characters saying these things, that I am not here but sitting at my desk in Molextrics, thinking these things, having stress-induced visions.

For example, now, something I am making a character say is something that I am wondering about. The character says, Racism is not the abomination, the concept of biologically distinct races is. But we have the knowledge now that blows all that categorisation nonsense out of the water. Genetics. DNA. The genetic material. How we are all jumbled reiterations, evolutions of genetic material.

Remember, I make another character say, on the American TV programmes, the police and detective programmes we grew up with, right into the nineteen seventies. The suspect is Caucasian, lieutenant. Can you ever remember hearing that language?

Ah, now! Language. Now we are talking, I make the race comment character say.

Well, I suppose languages are always changing. Scots and English, certainly, those two languages—

Those two languages? I make the other character say. Now I think you are making a political point that somebody somewhere ought to do something about!

You dispute that English and Scots are two languages?

No. I dispute that all languages are distinct in any way that makes sense. There is only language, that multiplicity of ways that human beings communicate with one another. As there are no races, there are no languages, just the jumble of genes of humans for the former and jumble of memes for the latter.

Nonsense!

Oh? Haven't you heard of language families? And let me remind you, families were how people viewed others, in families, before the scourge of thinking of them being in races became popular. Haven't you heard? English and Scots are in the same family, Indo-European, and evolved through the Germanic languages, to the West Germanic, to North Sea Germanic, Anglo-Frisian and Anglic. But these are just names. Words don't have meanings, they have etymology!

But… but Scots is distinct enough from English to be a language on its own.

You're not listening to me! There are no languages. Just Language. No literatures. Just Literature. You're talking politics, not reality.

Bu—

Jesus, think how poor our cultural life would be if it wasn't for nicking all things French? I mean, I like to head to a rendezvous for a liaison at a restaurant with an apéritif followed by some champagne and on to a menu of sliced baguette, then omelette, soufflé and salad with vinaigrette. After this we'll be chauffeured to watch one of these chic, risqué, avant-garde cabaret premières where we'll find the use of silhouettes all too easy to ridicule because it is too sentimental. We won't bother picking up the souvenir programme. You tell me about the nouveau roman novel you're reading that is an homage to film noir. As for debris on the streets around the theatre, what we need is a cordon sanitaire pour encourager les autres to clear up after themselves in the urban environs. Get your beret on, son, and bon voyage. Identity is an illusion redolent of the insult of irony. Now, tell me, muse, are these words English or Scots?

They're French.

You're not seeing my point. They're memes, free-floating around and ending up anywhere they can fit within language. Then this character continues incoherently, Great Vowel Shift, down through the centuries, goin to a waddin.

Memes, is it? I still say Scots is a language. It's my language.

That's politics, not linguistics, I make this character say.

Linguistics is politics in this country.

More than other countries? More than for the Basques? What you're talking about is *only* politics.

Aye? *Agus?* the other character replies.

And then, the strangest thing: the part of me that has been transcending time, my soul, my consciousness, my imagination, does finally take flight over the rooftops of Edinburgh, running wild along the ramparts of the Castle; some corporeal sense of myself must be present, as a guard presents his firearm and cries out, high-pitched, STAND STILL! But I am not corporeal enough, apparently, to be caught, to need to stand still, and I can move at will, faster and faster, skipping over Victoria as Britannia on top of the National Museum of Scotland, running through the Great Gallery in Holyrood Palace, passing the portraits of Scottish kings, more than half of them fake and almost all of them plagiarised by the painter, Jacob de Wet the Younger, in a lightning slapdash of two years for a hundred and eleven portraits, from George Jamesone, who picked up his nonsense list of kings of Scotland from the historian and tutor to a royal scion, George Buchanan, who had, at least, acknowledged much of the invalidity of his scholarship, admitted he freely made up what he did not know, and wrote decently enough elsewhere for the University of Oxford to bother to burn his books. I am looking at Buchanan now, on the west face, lower tier of the Sir Walter Scott Monument, a monument to the fake King of Scots letters, but also a towering monument to that other Scots fable, the inspired work of the self-taught son of the soil, in this case a chippie with a vision, born a shepherd's son, George Meikle Kemp, who pseudonymised his name as 'John Morvo' (lifted from the medieval architect of Melrose Abbey) to enter the competition to design the monument's exterior. It was a son of the gentry, though a family that had been shamed by bankruptcy and thus some-what shunned by the upright burghers of Edinburgh, John Steell, eventually Sir John Robert Steell RSA, who got to sculpt the actual centrepiece of the monument, Scott at toil with his dog at his feet, and there were sundry others who sculpted and carved the characters, imagined and historical, from Scott's books which adorn the monument. For a post-sixties generation, the resemblance to Thunderbird 3 is difficult to avoid. Half the masons who worked on the monument were dead soon after its completion, from what they knew as phthisis, as silicon pulmonary tuberculosis or silicosis to us, and as consumption to the poetic among us.

It's dry but cold out here on the streets. I'm flying close to the ground then up and around the monument. Michael, Chris and James, just out of school, stewards for the festivities, are standing talking among themselves, and Michael is wondering where Fred and Martin are. James knows and says, They're stationed in a pub at the top of Leith Walk. Bet they're warmer than us. Now I'm back in the Great Gallery of Holyroodhouse, passing the Tam o' Shanter Chair, made from oak light-fingeredly lifted from the roof of Alloway Auld Kirk, constructed by John Underwood of Ayr, then I'm back in the Castle, passing through the collection of the Crown Jewels and standing staring at the Stone of Scone, the Stone of

Destiny, twice-stolen, now returned to Edinburgh as of 1996. Now I am flying high up and straight down Castle Hill, the Royal Mile, sweeping past the Writers' Museum up Lady Stair's Close, where manuscripts by Burns and Scott and Stevenson ripple gently as I cause a disturbance in the air. I come to be at the heights above the city, on Arthur's Seat and Salisbury Crags, and now I am down at Ocean Terminal, Leith, up amongst the rigging of the foremast, mainmast and mizzenmast of Her Majesty's Yacht *Britannia*, the decommissioning ceremony where the Queen shed a tear the way she could not for a wayward ex-princess on my mind, and wondering why I have only come to Leith, not to near or at the site of John Brown and Company at Clydebank, where HMY *Britannia* was built alongside others, the Royal Mail Ships *Lusitania*, *Aquitania*, *Queen Mary*, *Queen Elizabeth* and *Queen Elizabeth II*, and Her Majesty's Ships *Repulse* and *Hood*, the last named for Admiral Samuel Hood, 1st Viscount Hood (12th December 1724–27th January 1816), who fought in battles at the time of the French and American Revolutionary Wars, and whose father, also Samuel Hood, was vicar of Butleigh in Somerset and prebendary of the Cathedral at Wells. Now I am up among the spires, the eight arched buttresses of the Crown Steeple of St Giles Cathedral, High Kirk of Edinburgh, looking down upon the Heart of Midlothian, where a passer-by happily hacks and spits, and on Calton Hill I run around the horizontal top stones of the ridiculous and unfinished National Monument of Scotland, memorialising the heroic Scots dead of the Napoleonic Wars and to incentivise the future pointless deaths in the same name of misguided heroism, Scotland's Folly, Edinburgh's Disgrace, the money ran out and the Napoleonic Wars got superseded by the horrors of

Passchendaele and Clydebank, while the Red Clydesider Thomas Johnstone pulled a fast one on Churchill by syphoning support and money to the Scottish Council for Industry and Clyde Basin Hospital Scheme, a proto-NHS which repurposed civilian-casualty-ready yet empty – as Hitler had turned his attention away from Clydebank and Greenock to Moscow, the one in Russia not East Ayrshire – set of well-equipped and well-staffed hospitals for the treatment of the common illnesses and injuries among the Scots working people caused by heavy industrialisation. Moscow in Ayrshire is named so, an altered spelling for the village's previous name, Mosshall – 'Moss-haw' in the local dialect – in honour of Napoleon's retreat from Moscow in 1812. I find myself, by flight and no doubt whimsy, back once more in the Little Kremlin room in Milne's, and Susan Alison and her people are nowhere to be seen, but Hugh MacDiarmid and Sydney Goodsir Smith, Robert Garioch, Edwin Morgan, George Mackay Brown, Iain Crichton Smith, Sorley Maclean and Norman MacCaig are all here, and I realise I'm not in an actual time and place but instead inside the painting by Alexander Moffat that adds in all the poets who reputedly drank in Milne's, though it's unlikely they all showed up on one night as depicted. For reasons I can't explain, all these writers are themselves and not their painted selves, as though this were the live-action sequel to the painted-animation original, and the poets are debating the overall legacy and individual legacies of Joseph Black and Adam Ferguson and Thomas Reid and of course David Hume and of course James Boswell and James Hutton and John Playfair and Dugald Stewart and William Cullen and of course Robert Burns and of course Adam Smith and Francis Hutcheson and whither the Union as a necessary precursor to the Enlightenment and of course

Allan Ramsay the poet and Allan Ramsay the painter and whither the French *Encyclopédie* as a necessary precursor to the first three-volume *Encyclopaedia Britannica*, the book that Edinburgh publishers produced as this monumental all-encompassing work of world knowledge, with a Britisher viewpoint rather than a French this time, but with the same aim as Diderot's, to democratise knowledge and alter for ever the way people understood the world and hence the way they *thought* and whither the Western Enlightenment led to the Scottish Enlightenment or vice versa or both or neither and James Beattie and George Turnbull and Hugh Blair and John Alexander and Robert Adam and his brothers and Thomas Erskine, 6th Earl of Kellie, and James Burnett, Lord Monboddo, and the tragedy of Robert Fergusson and of course James Macpherson of the Ossian fraud. Agreement is never reached. A fistfight is averted but only just.

Then I'm in the streets of Edinburgh, up and along Dundas Street, passing George Watson's College, James Gillespie's High School, the Free Church of Scotland's headquarters on the Mound, along Rodney Street in Canonmills, Balcarres Street in Morningside, past the statue of William Pitt the Younger in George Street, Charles the Second statue in Parliament Square, around the Georgian celebration of simplicity and angle of the roof of Dundas House and up and around the figure of Henry Dundas, Uncrowned King of Scotland, Great Tyrant, King Harry the Ninth, atop the column of the 1st Viscount Melville monument in St Andrew's Square and I'm behind MacDiarmid who's in St Andrew's Square to catch his bus back to Biggar with a glass of whisky in one hand and a cigarette in the other, these hands held out with Christ Crucified-like arms, high-wire skipping along, riding the kerbstones, and I realise I am yet again in an imagined time and place influenced by a number of thoughts and paintings and films. But here in the Café Royal, all there are are characters, movement and colour and form and shape and voices, voices, voices:

Lang may yur lum reek!

Aye, an a *cèilidh* inaw.

Davie Hume himself caud hisself North Briton.

Remember what he said, A rat race is for rats. We are not rats. We are human beings!

I'm writing a series of crime novels, set in Pittenweem.

Ian's in the Oxford. Said he was coming along, but he must have got stuck.

Oh, for God's sake, dinnae haver.

Fit a stramash!

Christ. Me heid's bealin.

What a weather it is!

The Declaration of Arbroath.

That bug won't bite.

Oi, pal. Oi, pal. Oi, PAL.

See me these days, I mean ye cannae, can ye? I jist think aboot the flooers these days, me.

Aw man, ye spilt ma pint.

Here, haud on. I am a long way from home.

You're wrong. Nationalism blinds you. Africans were being traded as slaves well before the transportation of Irish and Scots and Gypsies to the colonies.

You know they'll sell us down the river to achieve independence, don't you? They'll jettison everything that it was supposed to mean for us to get... what? They'll keep the monarchy, bow down or curtsy and kiss hands and arses, they'll keep pounds sterling, and therefore monetary union with the Bank of England. Pieces of silver right enough. They'll keep capitalism, encourage its growth, in fact. There's no socialist republic coming to us.

Are you talking of revolution?

I'm talking about the state of the nation.

Aye, the fuckin state of it!

TEN. NINE. EIGHT. SEVEN—
NAW. Ye're too soon!
SIX—
STOP! NOW!
TEN. NINE—
FIVE—
EIGHT—
FOUR—
SHUT IT—
SHUT IT—

THREE!—
STOP! STOP!
SIX—

Should auld acquaintance be forgot,
Should auld acquaintance be forgot,

And never brought to mind?
And never brought to mind?
Should auld acquaintance be forgot,

NOT YET.

Should auld acquaintance be forgot,
Should auld acquaintance be forgot,
And never brought to mind?

And auld lang syne?
And auld lang syne?
Should auld acquaintance be forgot,

For auld lang syne, my jo,
For auld lang syne, my jo,
And auld lang syne?

TOO SOON!

For auld lang syne,
For auld lang syne,
For auld lang syne, my jo,

We'll tak a cup o kindness yet,
We'll tak a cup o kindness yet,
For auld lang syne,

For auld lang syne
For auld lang syne
We'll tak a cup o kindness yet,

And surely ye'll be your pint-stowp!
And surely ye'll be your pint-stowp!
For auld lang syne

And surely I'll be mine!
And surely I'll be mine!
And surely ye'll be your pint-stowp!

And we'll tak a cup o kindness yet,
And we'll tak a cup o kindness yet,
And surely I'll be mine!

For auld lang syne.
For auld lang syne.
And we'll tak a cup o kindness yet,

For auld lang syne, my jo,
For auld lang syne, my jo,
For auld lang syne.

For auld lang syne,

We'll tak a cup o kindness yet,

For auld lang syne

We twa hae run about the braes

And pu'd the gowans fine;

But we've wander'd mony a weary foot

Sin auld lang syne.

For auld lang syne, my jo,

For auld lang syne,

We'll tak a cup o kindness yet,

For auld lang syne

We twa hae paidl'd in the burn,

Frae mornin sun till dine;

But seas between us braid hae roar'd

Sin auld lang syne.

For auld lang syne, my jo,

For auld lang syne,

We'll tak a cup o kindness yet,
We'll tak a cup o kindness yet,
For auld lang syne,

For auld lang syne
For auld lang syne
We'll tak a cup o kindness yet,

And there's a hand, my trusty fiere!
And there's a hand, my trusty fiere!
For auld lang syne

And gie's a hand o thine!
And gie's a hand o thine!
And there's a hand, my trusty fiere!

And we'll tak a right guid willy waught,
And we'll tak a right guid willy waught,
And gie's a hand o thine!

For auld lang syne.
For auld lang syne.
And we'll tak a right guid willy waught,

For auld lang syne, my jo,
For auld lang syne, my jo,
Sin auld lang syne.

For auld lang syne,
For auld lang syne,
For auld lang syne, my jo,

We'll tak a cup o kindness yet,
We'll tak a cup o kindness yet,
For auld lang syne,

For auld lang syne
For auld lang syne
We'll tak a cup o kindness yet,

Eh

10

15 seconds after

Whizzbangs and exploding light of the fireworks still going off, causing the walls and windows of the buildings of central Edinburgh to reflect the flowering hot embers, evanescence dying to senescence as ash falling through the air, to light up with a momentary daylight flash of whitened detail, and darkening the corners hidden from the light to black shadow, triple-perspectived, blurring at the edges as another firework goes off from this angle, then this, then this, the walls' corners' edges seem to shiver in the cold of the night. I am trembling, and my heart is exploding and my blood pressure is sky-high and my head is filled with whizzbangs, synapses and neurons gone wild.

From one of the pitch corners of the New College quadrangle a young man escapes clutches and runs from the arms of a man who calls, Will you phone me? If I've not to call you by your name or your title when we meet, the young man calls back, then what am I to call you? Patrick, says the man, coming into the light from here, from there, from here, over there. Call me Patrick when we meet again. He watches the young man turn a shivering corner then makes his way nonchalantly to the statue of the Reverend John Knox, whose fearsome visage is lit now this way, then that, then again another way. The many faces of Knox, the man is thinking, and there's a slight smile still playing upon his lips.

Is it too much to be unsurprised that this book filled with these characters about the beginning of the end of the world was of course set in Edinburgh? It's something about that statue of John Knox, isn't it? If any statue of an angry religious man was going to oversee the start of the end of the world, it would have to be him, the statue of him. Calvinism hit the weather, the miserable drizzle. Makes you pissy, being freezin all the time, always walking into the wind no matter what way you're facin.

I watch as the man looks up and stares into the face lit this way and that of Knox, and confesses. Like our friends in Saughton, he says, I'm a… prisoner of my deviancy, I am aberrant. I degrade my soul for a moment's madness. There is evil abroad and who will stare it in the face? You, John? Or myself? Still, on we go. On it goes. And ere long, I doubt, the country will be as free as the churches must be. There will be prayers and penance required. For me, and for you. Perhaps you should ponder what you did to our religion, and repent, John. What the Bishop of Dunblane would make of you I do not know.

He turns from the statue, pulls his coat about him and prepares to head home. As he walks out of the quadrangle he has to hold out his hands to stop a reveller from knocking him clean over and on to the pavement, perhaps even into the gutter, and he calls out, Please, madam, I was almost knocked off my feet!

Oh, Archbishop! she says, I *am* sorry!

Not to worry, he says quickly, this man, losing his breath, swallowing down his words, No harm done!

Oh, but I am so, so *sorry*, she says. And how unexpected to bump into you here!

Well, yes, the real action at Hogmanay is here in the streets, is it not? He makes to tear himself away from her, but she has grabbed his lapels. Drunk. The indignity of it!

What do you think, Father – will tonight give way to a good year?

He recoils as she seems to come close to kissing him. Ah, yes! he says. The millennium! Quite a night we have in store! But as to predictions, I always repeat what Alistair Cooke said about making New Year predictions.

And what was that, Archbishop?

He always used to say, every year, there will be trouble in the Middle East. And he was never proven wrong!

Ah, Father, you're reminding me of the good one I heard. I really must be going… I have a service—

Ah, away wae that, Father. You'll like this one.

If you're quick.

Aye, so, the word went out from some news agency, some UK agency, you know, just before the turn of the year and diplomats, diplomats for the UK, around the world, you know, they were asked what they were hoping for, for Christmas and the New Year, you see.

Yes, yes, I see.

And of course the replies started coming in. What was hoped for in this season of goodwill to all men… and women as well, of course.

Of course.

Was, you know, peace in the conflicts in their region, between rebels and governments, terrorists and police.

Of course, I see.

In South America… the Middle East… in… in… Russia and Mexico… the Philippines, I'm sure, was one of them…

I get the picture. I really must be—

Peace in the world, really, was what they were essentially saying. Peace in the world at this season… in this season of goodwill.

Isn't that nice… well…

NO! No! Wait, that's not it. You haven't had the punchline yet!

Oh, well, on you go.

So, anyway, haud yer horses, all right? So, anyway, this one little Eton mess somewhere in… I don't know, Kazakhstan or Uzbekistan… or maybe it was in Guyana or somewhere like that, he replies… he replies… he clearly hadnae got the memo, he says, obviously pining for the Christmas season of his pampered youth, when Nanny sorted him out, he says… ha…! he says, Some jellied sweets wouldn't go amiss! Do you get it, Father? Peace and happiness for the whole world and some jellied sweets wouldn't go amiss! Do you get it Father?

Quite so, quite so, but I really must be going now.

Pray for me, Father!

I'll pray for us all.

11

15 minutes after

Finally my heart rate goes down, at least a little, and I feel I can breathe again, in… out… in. The first things of the new year, decade, century, millennium have happened: the fireworks; the songs 'In Our Lifetime', 'When We Are Together', a sublime 'Halo', a tumultuous 'Drawing Crazy Patterns', sung by Sharleen Spiteri, her black Telecaster glinting, with Johnny and the band sounding massive and joyful; the ragged, mistimed, tuneless and sometimes tuneful versions of 'Auld Lang Syne' rising and falling; the shouts and screams and cries and laughter. The first calls of, C'mon, let's go. Haud on. And so we land back in time, and yet again the world has not ended. Thinking on it, why do we continually think the world is coming to an end when moment by moment, second by second, minute by minute, hour by hour, day by day, week by week, month by month, year by year, decade by decade, century by century, millennium by millennium it patently fails to come, the end? Is it because the actual end of everything only has to come once, whereas the continuation of everything has to happen over and over again?

I look around myself and realise I'm in Princes Street Gardens, not in the Café Royal any more. I'm at the concert that's put on each year – for the last few years, anyway – amongst the crowd within the closed-off area for the official celebrations of the New Year. Edinburgh has woken up to the way it can commodify its status as the premier New Year celebration venue, the place to be, the City of the New Year. It started, would you believe it, only in 1993. Perhaps it was the approaching millennium and the millennial build-up of those years, realising the biggest party in living collective human memory was on its way, something on the scale of watching the moon landings in 1969. 1992 was the last of the informal, ad-hoc parties outdoors in the streets of Edinburgh. If you wanted something apparently more formal, you'd be in London, listening for the chimes of Big Ben, watching fireworks going off, jumping into the freezing waters of the fountains in Trafalgar Square, though I say apparently, because actually until this year, six years after Edinburgh formalised arrangements, and three years after restrictions came in after the 1996 Edinburgh festivities attracted a dangerously uncontrolled 400,000 people, making a tragedy by crushing, stampede or other crowd dynamic all but inevitable if not addressed, these London celebrations have been similarly ad-hoc, informal gatherings of milling-about people. Mibby this has been sustainable because London simply has more space for those who want to stand around pointlessly on what is bound to be one of the colder nights of the year.

I'm back in time, in space, these dimensions, and the world has not ended. It won't be ending again until the next end of the world at 8, 9 A.M. on the 11th of September next year.

12

15 hours after

I wake up after three hours sleep, which comes after a twelve-hour bender, and this hangover feels like the end of the fuckin world. The day the earth still stood. My brother is on my mind as it, my mind, bends and warps on a rollercoaster ride which willnae stop goin roun an roun. He was explaining to me about the title of an Anthony Burgess novel he'd been reading, *The End of the World News*. He said it, the title, came about because one of the characters, or Burgess himself, used to listen to a Radio 4 or World Service programme at the end of each day called *The World News*. And every night the presenter would finish off the programme with the words, And that's the end of *The World News*…

I check the radio and the television. The nuclear arsenals have remained untriggered in their silos, in submarines, on the ground unattached to aircraft; the warheads within the ballistic missiles and bombs stayed piled wherever they are stockpiled. The financial markets have not crashed. And I have a message on my Molectrophone, recorded at some point as I slept, telling me that all is well within the networks and products of the company, which the full functioning of my Molectrophone conspires to confirm.

So, there you go, another end of the world just like the last end of the world. And just like the next end of the world to come.

13

15 days after

At Molextrics I clear my desk, disconnect myself from networks, discontinue my e-mail address: no need for a visionary who does nothing at all. I could make myself useful. Perhaps I could do some good at Molextrics: use my new-found ability to manipulate time, though only on millennium night so far, or my post-visionary ability to prophesy (a single instance and as yet not proven).

I get a piece of cake, a glass of fizz, a few desultory and generic words of farewell. I worked on my own, mostly: they don't know me. I'm sure they think I did nothing about the Y2K bug. I know I did nothing, so I win.

Mole isn't late. He's in the Caribbean and a complete no-show.

14

15 weeks after

Mole personally hands me the cheque for my bonus. I open the envelope and say, This is… extremely generous!

You deserve it. Whatever it is you did, Mole says, and winks.

I… I don't know what to say. I do have one question.

Oh?

You know what it is.

Sandy, Mole says, Long-term, there's room for *one* visionary in a company…

15

15 months after

My Wikipedia hyperlinks today:

Mole empire
Smollet & Sons
tobacco and sugar trade
Glasgow
the Caribbean
slave trading

ASSOCIATED PRESS WIRE: CONFIRMED MOLEXTRICS
NETWORKS FAILURE AT 00:00:00001, 31.12.00/01.01.01 DID
WIPE HALF BILLION OFF SHARE VALUE.

16

15 years after

Doomscrolling through headlines

Don the tractor driving dog safe at home

Mighty Murray mints Dunblane joy with marriage

Sturgeon's new political landscape

Gold and white or blue and black leaves family black and blue

We interview tractor driver Don to find out the twoof

Scotland's biggest New Year hangover since the millennium?

Is a Scottish golf-course owner really in the running for Prez?

Bin lorry tragedy investigation continues

Comedian Janey Godley says she'll do something funny for Trump's visit

Can you solve the crocodile conundrum?

above clickbait.

16

15 years after

Greetin!
#Jockalypse #Jimaggedon @NicolaSturgeon
#GE2015hangover #56seats #landfuckingslide #indyref2